I0642088

Mrs. Burton Harrison

Sweet Bells out of Tune

Mrs. Burton Harrison

Sweet Bells out of Tune

ISBN/EAN: 9783743305274

Manufactured in Europe, USA, Canada, Australia, Japa

Cover: Foto ©Andreas Hilbeck / pixelio.de

Manufactured and distributed by brebook publishing software
(www.brebook.com)

Mrs. Burton Harrison

Sweet Bells out of Tune

"HE IS WAITING FOR ME."

SWEET BELLS OUT OF TUNE

BY MRS. BURTON HARRISON

AUTHOR OF " THE ANGLOMANIACS," " CROW'S NEST AND
BELHAVEN TALES," ETC.

WITH ILLUSTRATIONS BY

C. D. GIBSON

NEW YORK: THE CENTURY CO.

1893

LIST OF ILLUSTRATIONS

SWEET BELLS OUT OF TUNE

I

BURST of fortissimo music from the organ, which had been dawdling over themes from Wagner's operas, caused every head in the seated congregation to turn briskly around. Some people stood up, swaying to catch a first glimpse of the bride. Outsiders, tucked away in undesirable back-pews, went so far as to scramble upon the cushioned seats.

It was, however, a false alarm. The middle aisle, center of interest, developed nothing more striking than a trim little usher, in pearl gloves with a buttonhole of white carnations, convoying to her place of honor beyond the ribbon a colossal lady with auburn front, red in the face, and out of breath.

Conversation in pews reserved for the elect of good society.

She: "Hum! Bridegroom's maiden aunt, suppressed generally—how Freddy rushes her along! Sent twelve silver soup-plates and a huge tureen, when everybody knows soup is served from behind

1

the screen, and it would take all one servant's time to keep 'em clean — but she thinks she 's paid her way well to the front, poor soul!"

He: "Here 's the groom's mother — deuced fine woman yet is Mrs. Vernon. Who 'd believe she 'd a son of five-and-twenty? Hates to admit it publicly, but is putting on the best face she can."

She: "Not her best face — her second best. I 've seen her improve on that. But then, this half daylight, half electricity is abominably trying. And she really does look *very* well, viewed from the rear."

He: "Clever, too — the way she 's run the family up — when one thinks what the husband was."

She: "Does one ever think of him? By the way, what was he — soldier, sailor, tinker, tailor, what?"

He: "Tinker, most likely, considering the family brass. I saw him once — coarse-grained creature, epidermis like an elephant, diamond in his shirt-front, and all that. Speculated after the war in Virginia City mines, and made a big fortune; then dropped dead of apoplexy, and left it for her to spend. She sent her boy to a good school; gave with a free hand to all the charities; boy made friends everywhere; went through Harvard like a streak; has traveled, yachted, hunted, been in the best sets ever since; is about to marry into one of the proudest of the exclusive families of New York — and there you are."

She: "Oh! But he 's really such a beauty, don't you know? Half the women in town have been pulling caps for Jerry Vernon. And, after all, what are the Hallidays but has-beens?"

He: "Take care. There 's one of their high-born

ramifications glaring at you from the next pew—old lady with eye-glasses and a sniff. Came up from Second Avenue in a horse-car—looks like the unicorn on the British coat of arms."

She: "Gracious! It's the bride's cousin or something; let's change the subject. Oh! *did* you hear poor Mrs. Jimmie Crosland could n't go to the opera last night because that wretched, jealous husband shut her nose in a wardrobe door?"

He: "Really? Was n't theirs the last wedding we came to in this church?"

She: "Of course. Don't you remember? Regular peep-show; six chorus girls from the opera, in white veils, to sing 'The voice that breathed o'er Eden.' They say she even hired the pages to hold up her train—put 'em in Charles II. wigs, and passed 'em off for little brothers."

He: "Exactly. One gets these theatrical affairs so confoundedly mixed up. See, the groom's mother is still upon her knees. A woman could n't pray so conspicuously unless in back seams from Worth."

She: "For shame! How malicious you men are! I should have said it's because she's keeping Mrs. Vane-Benson standing in the aisle for every one to see. You know they have been at some trouble to corral relatives to match the bride's, and Mrs. Vane-Benson's their trump card. How bored the poor rector looks waiting in his bower of palms."

He: "Queer how people marry, and bury, and flirt, under palm-trees, nowadays! I'm getting awfully tired of being tickled by the spiky things every time I sit out a dance, or go to call upon a girl. Hullo!

There 's Mrs.—what does she call herself since she got her divorce ?"

She (animated): "Is she? No, really? I would n't have missed seeing Hildegarde de Lancey for the world. It 's the first time she 's been out. Is n't she perfectly lovely in that gray bengaline and chinchilla, with the bunch of violets at her breast? I always did say Hildegarde—*de Lancey* she is now; so nice to have got rid of her odious, ugly Smithson—is the best-dressed woman in this town. Why, what a belle she is! I believe all the ushers would like to escort her in a body up the aisle. Of course Freddy de Witt saved her a front place. He knows what people want to see."

He: "She 's a charmer, certainly. If I were the Mrs. Gerald Vernon that is soon to be, I 'd be rather glad Mrs. de Lancey is proposing to live abroad."

She: "Oh, nonsense. You men always think the worst. Jerry was touched, no doubt, but Hildegarde meant nothing. You can't conceive of a greater brute than Smithson, and Hilda was always such a darling thing. Every one says she is in luck to get rid of him so soon. How well she looks—no wonder everybody stares. Oh, I 'm so glad we 're to have Hilda back!"

Elsewhere in the church.

A mother in Israel to her young daughters: "So that 's the famous divorcée, Mrs. What 's-her-name Smithson, the papers have been so full of lately? Don't look at her, Doris and Gladys; I insist that you don't look that way. Have you observed the figure of Dorcas in poor Mrs. Golding's memorial window?

The drawing of the right arm is excellent—I wonder if *that person* does anything to her hair to give it that baby gold. I would n't trust her any farther than I could see. Dear me! the best people bowing, and smirking, and trying to catch her eye. Ahem! Mrs. de Lancey's toque sits quite close to the head, girls; I think it much more becoming than those great cart-wheel hats you insisted upon having sent home."

Doris and Gladys: "We know, mama; we 've been watching her ever since she came into the church. What fun it must be to make as much stir as the bride!"

Two girls in tailor gowns, with fur boas and muffs. They have come in an omnibus to the nearest corner, and were splashed with mud in getting out.

"Dear me! we *are* lucky, but I had to push awfully to squeeze in. If I had n't known Tom Brownlee, I 'd have never had this seat. He asked me if we are going on to the house, and I coughed and smiled, and he took it to mean yes. My, Jennie, look at the new suits! I can tell you the names of 'most everybody here. I do know the bride, anyhow, for we 're on a working-girl's amusement board, together. I must say she 's as nice a girl as I ever wish to meet. Can't say as much for her sister, Miss Betty—such a lank, sour-looking thing, and a tongue sharp as a razor. Nobody can stand her in our club. I wish the organ would n't play so loud you can't hear yourself talk. Gracious, child! lean over, and let me take that lump of mud off your face. I 'm thinking I can alter my blue Henrietta cloth by putting coat-tails bound with velvet on the basque, like the one that 's just gone by.

1*

Have a chocolate, do ; got 'em fresh to-day, as I passed
by Tyler's, on my way to match my blue.   Oh ! I *do*
love weddings.   I go to every single one I can."

Lady from the Faubourg St. Stuyvesant, seated
well forward in the church.

" Poor Margaret Halliday ! there she comes with
Betty and Trix and Jack.   I wonder if her grandfather is n't turning in his grave at this minute, over
the marriage of a Halliday with one of these upstart
Vernons.   Humph !   Margaret looks haggard, Betty
as yellow as a pumpkin, Trix rather overblown, and
Jack growing up one of the beefy kind.   I 'm glad it
is n't *my* daughter who 's to be sacrificed, that 's all."

Lady, who has secured end of pew on aisle, whisper-
ing to her husband next to her.

" George, that 's Mrs. Clarkson that edged by you
just now.   If you 'd known it, you 'd surely have been
more polite.   ' Who in the dickens *is* Mrs. Clarkson,
anyway ? '   When we met them at dinner at the Tomp-
kins', and you took her in, and were so charmingly
agreeable !   I declare, if I 'd had the least idea you
were going to be glum and cross at a wedding, I 'd
never have persuaded you to come.   ' Enough for you
to have had to shell out the sixth pair of piano-candle-
sticks this year, without boring yourself with the wedding too ! '   *George !*   You know you were always fond
of Nellie Halliday.   *Please* try, only try—I don't say
you will succeed—to be a *little bit* like other people.
I have given up hoping for *more* when you go out
with me."   (Mrs. Clarkson just then engaging George
in conversation, he becomes easy and smiling on the
spot.)

Two Hibernian ladies, in silk gowns and imitation cashmere shawls, are ushered into the seats reserved for the domestics of both families.

"Arrah now, it 's a sad day, Misthress Branigan, an' you that 's cuk in it only this twelvemonth can't tell the faylins o' me, that raised me little Nellie from a four-year-old; the light o' the house goes out wid her, the darlint. 'Go, Norah,' says she, pushin' me wid her two honds like swan's-down, 'be off wid ye to the church, an' sthop yer cryin', to watch yer gyirl come oop the aisle in all her finery.' 'An' is it happy ye are, Miss Nell?' says I. 'Norah,' says she, wid a little swate smile in the eyes of her, 'if it 's the last word I have to spake to me old nurse before I 'm med Misthress Vernon, I 'm that happy *I 'm afraid.*'"

Duet in the vestry. Jerry Vernon and his best man, Dick Henderson.

The bridegroom: "Oh, but I say, old man, something 's happened at the house, or in the street, or—hang it, you need n't grin. Look at the soles of these boots, will you? If that infernal fellow of mine has n't been and put a brand-new pair on me, after all; and all the ushers and bridesmaids will be grinning when we kneel down. Don't you think the rector could be induced to bless us *standing up?* I 'd double the fee, or—anything. Dick, if an accident has happened to that girl—this is a judgment on me for jeering at those who went before—I never heard such a bally old idiot as that organist—he makes me fairly crazy with his jigging tunes—you 're sure you 've got the ring?—ridiculous little object to cause all this fuss, is n't it?—Nell wears a six glove, and

look at the height of her—I never could have married
a little woman—by Jove, Dick, I wish we two did n't
have to amble in there before everybody and simper
at the crowd. *What? Coming?* Back me up, Dick,
and I 'll go at it like a man. Nell 's worth it, every
time."

Among the ushers huddled in the vestibule. The
weary Mr. Frederic de Witt, mopping his beaded
brow :

" Dumping the bridesmaids outside, are they ? Well,
I 'm glad. Great Cæsar ! but I 'm tired. The cheek
of women at weddings, and the push ! No ; I decline
to see any reporter. I refuse to divulge where they
are going for the wedding journey, the names of those
here present, or the price Jerry paid for our scarf-pins.
You gave Jerry notice in the vestry, did you ? Hope
you did n't forget to remind him that the unfortunate
man, having partaken of a light breakfast of eggs,
bread, and coffee, usually walks with a firm step to
the place of execution. Hi, there, gentlemen ! Fall
into line to precede the bridesmaids, if you please."

Among the bridesmaids.

" If we look as well as the couple that walk before
us, I 'm all right. These directoire hats and coats are
certainly too sweet. Oh ! are n't you scared to death ?
But it 's better than being Nell."

The bride (divinely tall and most divinely fair—a
rose flush in her cheeks, her dark lashes downward
bent, her dark hair knotted low on her neck, the old
lace of her mother's bridal veil like frost-work upon
her trailing robes of white, no ornament but a string
of pearls around her throat, one of her hands lightly

laid on the arm of the respectable old cousin who has been haled from his respectable old club to do parental duty for the day), to herself:

"I saw him. He is waiting for me. All these people are here to see me become Jerry's wife. But it makes no difference. If we were in a desert it would be just the same. The thought of him fills my whole heart. I wonder if it 's selfish and wicked to care for nothing, now, but the joy and the glory of being Jerry's wife."

"Until death us do part." The troth plight was interchanged; Jerry's hand, colder than her own, put the ring upon her finger; and the rector, who had baptized Eleanor, pronounced them man and wife.

During the ceremony the lower part of the church, having sated its curiosity, was in full buzz of chat about the plainness of the bride's gown, the absence of diamonds reputed to have been given by the groom, and the question whether guests should go on to the reception at once, or amuse themselves with other occupations of the hour.

While the clergyman was in the act of pronouncing the benediction, and the organist was panting to let himself loose on the wedding-march from "Lohengrin," people were buttoning their wraps, and gliding out of the church, to be sure of their carriages before the crush. Hardly had Eleanor passed under the awning to her carriage—and to the reality of life—before public interest in the bride had in a great measure exhaled.

But they rallied around her presently in the house occupied by Mrs. Halliday and her daughters, looking into a quiet down-town square. The wide double drawing-rooms of the old family mansion had put aside their shadows for the day. Under an arch of greenery and lilies Eleanor received her friends, Gerald at her side, looking quite pitiably conscious and ill at ease.

The bridesmaids, headed by Trix, Nell's eighteen-year-old sister, to whom this event was a species of début into society, stood in a semicircle, wearing the expression of amateur actors who have just acquitted themselves of a performance in which they happily believe the rest of the world to have been as much interested as were they. The crowd, jostling forward to pay salutation to bride and groom, continued afterward to jostle on general principles. Exchanging inquiries to which no one listened for the answer, and comments as to the nicety of having one of the old-school houses open again for entertainment, they then pushed on to the dining-room to partake, less enthusiastically, of an old-school collation marked by the absence of terrapin and truffles, and by the limited amount of the champagne. From the walls of this refectory looked down a row of oil-paintings in faded frames of gilt; a spirited young man with a Henry Clay stock and standing collar, flanking a high-colored lady in a bonnet with a bird-o'-paradise, and a scarf over her bare shoulders; sundry Continental soldiers, New England Brahmins, and a stiff-busked dame or two of remoter date, with attendant cavaliers in periwigs and ruffles. Over the sideboard hung a sour-visaged personage of Revolutionary date, the great-grandfather of the bride, familiarly spoken of among his descendants as "The Signer." He was a strong tower of American aristocracy, and Mrs. Halliday always felt that in his protecting presence at her parties she could venture to order in another bottle or so of soda-water to dilute her champagne punch. Everywhere in the house thus brought to contemporaneous notice there were marks of gentility that lacked repair. The hangings and furniture, placed there before the century's new birth into righteousness of taste, were massive but shabby. The carpets, worn into threadbare spots ill-concealed by modern rugs—the walls, faded beyond hiding with palms and rubber-trees sent in (on close contract) by the florist—called aloud for restoration. Although it was the fashion to say, when glancing casually about these rooms, "How delightful! How solid! What relief after the varnish and glitter of up-town!" no one was observed to linger there over long, or to return unless especially bidden to a function of exigent conventionality. This afternoon, in custody of a band of hirelings, who before cockcrow of another dawn would vanish, bearing with them every spoon, fork, plate, and glass now in service for the guests, the premises did not suggest even their usual homely comfort.

But to-day, for the first time in many days, Mrs. Halliday's handsome features wore a look of complacent satisfaction. Betty, the eldest daughter, aged six-and-twenty, plain, angular, and pessimistic, stood by her mother at the door of the drawing-room, outside of which was posted Andrews, the lean, old-time butler, to announce the guests. Jack, the collegian, tall and pink-cheeked, with a down on the upper lip that his sister Trix thought wonderful, a little too conscious of a new frock-coat with its buttonhole of gardenias, wandered about incessantly, resenting the notice of his mother's old friends who told him how much he had grown, and repudiating suggested resemblance to this or that portrait upon the walls. In the rear of the two ladies was a man, no longer in his first youth, of distinguished though inconspicuous presence —a man with sleepy gray eyes and a languid manner, before whom Betty was always at her best.

"My dear Anthony," his hostess had said to him, "you are at home here; you know everybody; for Heaven's sake, stay and help me out with Nell's 'in-laws.'"

"My dear cousin, I am yours as always," he had responded, with a smile, not however mirthful.

"The list is fortunately short," whispered Betty in mocking tones. "Here, mother, comes your very largest pill—Nell's new mama."

"Yes, everything has gone off well. I am pleased that you admire the lace. No, my daughter is not tired; we have not allowed her to do much." Mrs. Halliday was conscious of her thin, cold voice, and felt that it was a poor return for Eleanor's new house, horses, brougham, victoria, not to mention the necklace and solar system in diamonds, already at the Safety Deposit Company's, in waiting till the bride's return from her wedding journey,—the last Gerald's gift, paid for by Mrs. Vernon's check. But Mrs. Vernon was quite beyond the point of sensitiveness on the trifling score of measured civilities. Ensconced as a relative within these shabby walls, she felt that

"WE ARE BEHIND TIME, MRS. VANE-BENSON AND I."

her price was far above rubies or diamonds either! If Jerry had to put upon her the indignity of being a prospective grandmother, he had at least done it in good form.

"We are behind time, Mrs. Vane-Benson and I," she said, as the lady named made her bow, and retired to mingle with the throng; "but Mrs. Vane-Benson judged it would be more the thing for us to let the young people—such children! but I, myself, was married at sixteen—get a little settled down before I fluster them with my congratulations; and I told her I guessed she was right."

Mrs. Halliday winced at the voice and speech. She hardly dared trust herself to look full in the face this modish person in silver-gray with silver broideries, with the silver bonnet perched on her dark, glossy locks, with the brilliant color softened by rice-powder, the dazzling teeth, the frequent laugh, the effusive cordiality, the aroma of prosperity. She became conscious of lines in her own face, and of a break under her chin, that ought to have been, but were not, in Mrs. Vernon's. She looked down at her old black velvet supplied with a new frontispiece of jetted lace, and marked the contrast between its indescribable wispiness and the crisp perfection of Mrs. Vernon's attire. Altogether, she was in some haste to rid herself of dear Eleanor's mama.

"You will be wanting to speak to Nell and Gerald," she said. "Mr. Theobald will give you his arm across the rooms—Anthony—my cousin Mr. Theobald, Mrs. Vernon."

The hazel eyes took on a new luster of delight. To

be translated into the heart of that inner circle that till now she had only "brushed with extremest flounce" was to cross the room leaning on the arm of "my—why not 'our'?—cousin Mr. Theobald."

To Theobald, for reasons of his own, the whole affair was a somewhat grim comedy; and, abandoning himself to the situation, he duly brought the widow to a halt before the bridal pair.

"My dearest Jerry—my sweetest Nell," the lady said, embracing both with such exuberance that Gerald fidgeted.

"We shall see more of each other now," Eleanor said, very low. "Gerald has told me of all your generosity; he thinks there was never a mother so kind as his."

"Gerald knows I shall be terribly alone," began the older woman, tears ready to twinkle in her eyes.

"Madre, you must n't, please," the young fellow whispered, in a tumult of alarm. With Freddy de Witt, Henderson, and the others looking on, he felt that an expansion of maternal tenderness would be his death-blow.

"Mrs. Vernon will perhaps allow me to take her into the dining-room," interposed Mr. Theobald, from the bride's elbow, where he had been standing without speech.

"So polite of you, dear Mr. Theobald," exclaimed flattered Madame Mère, linking her arm again in his.

The danger was averted. Nell, who, better than any other, knew Theobald's fastidious taste, flashed on him a quick glance of gratitude. She reproached herself, when he had gone, that she had not said something in the way of personal thanks for his gift of the etchings, so long coveted, which had arrived that morning framed for her boudoir in the new home. And now her attention was claimed by a radiant personage who was for the first time a guest beneath their roof.

"It was more than I hoped, to make your acquaintance in this way," said Hildegarde de Lancey. "Mr. Vernon and I have always been such chums."

Eleanor blushed, remembering the little passage-at-arms with her mother regarding this lady's name upon Jerry's list. She sent a swift inquiring look — the gaze of a "young-eyed cherub" fortified with innocence — into the pair of blue orbs that met hers with a deprecating, almost pathetic appeal. Certainly, such an ingenuous beauty could not be to blame for her undue share of human griefs.

"We are glad to welcome you," the bride said graciously.

"Every one is so good to me," murmured Hildegarde, with exquisite pathos.

"And Gerald says you have been so good to him," went on Eleanor, while Jerry's attention was absorbed by some one else.

"It is his grateful nature, as you will find. But I am keeping back your friends, so *au revoir*," and the vision disappeared.

"Jerry, she's exquisite," said Eleanor.

"Who is?—there are so many shes. Nell, here's my Aunt Tryphena, who sent us—by Jove, what did she send? Never mind; thank the old girl profusely, and choke her off—good luck a man don't have to gush over apostle-spoons and salt-cellars every day of the year."

2

"O NELL, it must be so nice to be you," cried Trix, presently, when, in their bedroom, she hovered around her sister, helping old Norah to put on the bride's frock for traveling. "This sable cape Aunt Penfold sent is simply gorgeous. Betty says she'd have given mink, if you had married a poor man. And Jerry's so good-looking, and such a dear—hurry, Nell, everybody's in the hall, and Jerry and Jack are fussing, declaring you'll miss the train—oh! I've been having a peep out of the window at your new brougham, lined with dark myrtle-green satin such as we've always dreamed of—such horses, such rugs, and such a big, big footman to tuck you in and touch his hat—no more cabs by the hour for you, you lucky girl."

"Run, now, you silly Trix, and tell Jerry I'll be there, and ask mama to come; and you, Norah dear, take that long face away and don't let me see it till you've learned to smile. Mama, are we alone? May I lock the door? Good-by, darling, *darling;* and would you mind sitting down upon this little chair, and letting me say my prayer at your knee, just to ask God to make me fit for such *perfect* happiness?"

II

Y dear Miss Halliday," wrote Mrs. Vernon to the sister of her new daughter-in-law, a few days after the young couple had left town on their wedding journey, "Will you and your sister Beatrix give me the great pleasure of your company at an early dinner, very informally, at seven o'clock on Wednesday next, to go afterward to the opera? I am asking your cousins Mr. Thomas Halliday and Mr. Theobald; and, with the exception of one other man, we shall be quite a family party. I am longing for an opportunity to talk over with you the first news from our darling wanderers. Believe me, yours faithfully, M. VERNON. Thursday."

"'M. Vernon, Thursday'—humph! Signs herself like a duchess; her name 's Martha Luella Ann," observed Betty, throwing the note upon the table in the up-stairs sitting-room where the ladies Halliday were wont to read, sew, write notes, discuss their friends, and dictate to the day-dressmaker. "Family party, indeed! I knew we 'd be plunged into a bosom friendship. I don't believe Anthony Theobald would be *caught* at a Vernon dinner."

19

"Oh, yes, he would," cried Trix, coming in equipped for a walk with her fox-terrier around the square. "I saw him after the play last night, looking wretched, really; and he asked me if we are going, and said he will be there."

"Then I suppose you approve of our making friends with Mammon?" said Betty to her mother. "Don't you think it 's enough for Nell to have set up her golden calf? Why can't we grovel in honest pauperism, and maintain our self-respect?"

"My dear Betty!" said Mrs. Halliday, compressing her lips resignedly. She had long ago given up entering the lists of discussion with her eldest daughter.

"I want to go," said Trix, stoutly. "I 'm dying to see one of Mrs. Vernon's dinners, and to go to the opera under the shadow of her new tiara. The newspapers say it 's a second-hand crown of real royalty, bought at a Paris sale."

"Well, her man is waiting, so make up your minds," resumed Betty, sitting down at the davenport, and dipping her pen in ink. "If the senders of invitations could hear the bickering they cause in families, I don't think society would go on with such a rush. So you *insist* on our accepting, mother?"

"Not at all," answered Mrs. Halliday, plucking up spirit. "Trix may, for we must keep in with Nell's new people; but you will, as usual, do exactly as you please."

"It may end—who knows?—in Jerry's Aunt Tryphena chaperoning us to a Patriarchs'," murmured Betty, dashing off, as she had intended to do since hearing that Theobald was to be of the party, a smooth acceptance of Mrs. Vernon's courtesy. "I like 'our darling wanderers,'—as if they were lost dogs!"

To end the conversation, Mrs. Halliday took up a newspaper addressed to her through the mail, and tore from it the cover. Trix, departing with the note and the terrier, did not see the white look that came upon her mother's face, or hear the stifled exclamation of dismay uttered by the poor lady as she dropped the journal in her lap.

"What in the world ails you, mother?" began Betty.

"Oh! this is infamous," cried her mother. "Take it away. I refuse to read another word—mixing up my daughter's name with the scandal about that de Lancey woman's divorce. Betty, if Nell were to see this, it would break her heart. Oh! if her father had been alive, they would never have dared—of course it is all a wretched lie about Jerry and Mrs. Smithson. Jerry asked for her invitation, and Jerry is a gentleman, at least. Betty, I've no patience with you, standing there like a stock."

For Betty, quite mistress of herself, had picked up, smoothed out, and was reading the offending article with a scornful little smile. It was one of those upas-like exotics of modern society journalism, a two-column account of the Vernon-Halliday nuptials, with side-issues of biography of all concerned, set forth with plentiful cheap wit, audacious statement, and deadly innuendo. After disposing in short order of the bridegroom's pretensions to social importance, and affecting to voice the surprise of good society that the bride's family should have so frankly displayed

2*

its inability to resist a golden bait, it went on to give
at length the history of Mr. Gerald Vernon's late well-
known infatuation for "our most recent and distinguished divorcée."

"That 's a fin-de-siècle phrase," quoth Betty, coolly,
laying down the journal without an added tinge upon
her cheek. "My dear little mammy, don't take the
thing so hard. Everybody will read it, of course, and
enjoy it thoroughly."

"Betty, how can you? I shall have to leave town,
certainly. I remember when I danced with the Prince
of Wales at the Academy ball, and my dress was de-
scribed next day in the papers, your dear father was
so vexed, he wanted to go and overhaul the editor.
Our family could never bear to see women in print—
oh! we shall not be able to face the light of day. It
is bad enough to drag in this wretched Mrs. Smithson,
but imagine the outrage of saying Nell's f-father-in-
law married her m-mother-in-law from the *wash-tub!*
Did you ever hear of such an abominable charge?"

"No—o," answered Betty. "I always thought it
was from a beauty-show. The wash-tub, now, seems
to me quite an advance in the social scale. Mother
dear, bear up. By the time you meet the people you
know again, they will have forgotten all about it.
This kind of pillory in print is too common in our
society to hurt anybody long. In next week's issue
of this charming sheet you may no doubt have the
pleasure of seeing some hit at the people who this
week laugh at you. Here, see me poke the wretched
thing into the hottest part of the fire; and you take
Trix, and go out for a week to Lakewood."

"But Nell,—my darling, sensitive Nell,—suppose she reads this cruel paragraph."

"I'm not in the least afraid of Nell seeing anything but the light that lies in Jerry's eyes, for—I will give her till the end of the honeymoon before taking up human interests again. If Jerry sees it, he will probably whistle and say a good many bad words. If Mrs. Vernon sees it, it will do her good. That kind of woman needs a little rap over the knuckles from time to time, to keep her in her place."

"Betty!" said Mrs. Halliday. She often felt that there was a sort of monotony in these monosyllabic rejoinders to her daughter's trenchant sentences.

Mrs. Vernon's dinner was distinctly a success. To meet Betty and Trix she had convened old Mr. Tom Halliday, the cousin without reproach, who, it will be remembered, had given Eleanor away at the altar; Mr. Theobald, and an extremely nice young Southerner, whose father had been killed in the war, and whose family was supposed to go back in an unbroken line to William the Conqueror, like all other Virginians, present or to come. To this Mr. Brockenborough Vyvan, a broad-shouldered, soft-voiced youth, Trix was assigned, and while secretly wondering where Mrs. Vernon had got him, the little minx was taking his measure and deciding that he pleased *her*, which, happily, is all a healthy girl in her first season generally cares to ascertain. Betty, going in with Theobald, was eminently suited and almost amiable. Old Tom, seated at Mrs. Vernon's right, fell into a doze after the first entrée, but waked up every time the servant

appeared at his elbow with a new dish, and, for the
rest, let the widow talk in a constant stream—which
led her to declare to his young cousins afterward that
he was really one of the most agreeable "dinner men"
in town.

The dining-room, hung with tapestries and opening
into a great conservatory, the perfection of plate, porcelain, wines, and service were noteworthy, even in
extravagant New York. Betty, recalling, as under
such circumstances guests inevitably will, the story
of Mrs. Vernon's origin, and her recent struggles for
social recognition, marveled at the ease, even ele-
gance, with which she now presided. She could not,
at a bird's-eye view, behold much difference between
this and a similar dinner before the opera a few
nights ago, in the penetralia of good society. She
remembered having heard some one say that "poor
Mrs. Vernon had had absolutely no chance while her
husband lived—a crass vulgarian, sure to put his foot
into everything; a typical American, like a commercial advertisement at the back of a magazine." The
time lost in mourning him had been spent by the
widow abroad, and in bringing up his son. And it
was not till Gerald left college, and got in with the
mothers and sisters of his fashionable friends, that
the Vernons actually came up for notice. Even then,
he was invited, she ignored. The great fine house,
into which she did not choose to bid the half-way
people who would have been glad to go, was like a
prison, in dreariness. Jerry's men came and went to
and from his suite of rooms on the third floor, but
never put in an appearance in his mother's drawing-

room. This, at least, was what Betty Halliday had heard. She saw that on the wave of Jerry's marriage into one of the "really good old" families Mrs. Vernon had resolved to ride into the haven of her hopes. And Betty could not but admit that she was doing this thing with a good deal of cleverness.

"What an exchange from our shabby house to such splendor!" remarked Betty, in a low tone. "I 'm rather glad Nell is to have a more modest establishment of her own. One can never keep up a friendship with riches that slap you in the face."

"She is the one woman I ever saw who would always, rich or poor, be herself," Theobald said, and then, relapsing into his usual impassive manner, turned the talk into another channel. "Speaking of homes, the site of this is where the old Sydney Wardour house used to stand ; and twenty years ago it was a center of hospitality in New York, and accounted the height of fashion. How homely their entertainments would seem beside such as these, and how cramped their quarters ! "

"What has become of the Sydney Wardours ?" said Betty. "One rarely hears their name."

"What has become of all our once prominent families of moderate wealth who are submerged in the flood-tide of plutocracy? Either broken to pieces in the attempt to keep up, or the heads of the families dead, and the younger ones reduced to insignificance."

"The way we live now certainly does n't incline one to indifference to wealth," she said. "The young men I know are most of them on the *qui vive* to help along their fortunes by a rich marriage ; and as to the girls, it is no longer a support they expect from their husbands, but unlimited opportunity."

"Then it is well a woman like Hildegarde de Lancey comes a cropper now and then, to point a moral for the rest."

"I don't see what you call coming a cropper," retorted Betty, scornfully. "She is more in demand than any one I know — in the smart set, I mean. Old-fashioned people like my mother hold up their hands, but society — our society, *the* society — caresses her, and condones what they are pleased to call her misfortunes. She is immensely in the swim. She was the bright star of a dinner the other night at the Bullions', where six out of the twelve guests are living apart from their legal partners, owing to infelicities too numerous to cite."

"By Jove, we are catching up with Chicago," said Theobald. "Did you see the squib in one of the papers recently, where an English traveler asks Mrs. Lakeside if she has been presented yet at court? 'My gracious! yes, indeed,' she answers; 'every judge in the city knows me; I've been divorced three times.'"

"Tony, tell me something," Betty pursued more gravely. "You must know how people talk. Is there any reason why Nell should — no; I can't ask you here. But I think we can count upon you to keep us warned. One don't want to be made a fool of before the world; and you know you always were so fond of Nell."

Theobald drank off at a draught his newly filled tazza of champagne before he answered, with a laugh:

"I think Mrs. de Lancey will find it to her advantage to keep quiet for a while. Let us talk of something pleasanter—Trix, for instance. That tête-à-tête with the athletic youngster yonder does n't promise well for the chances of Mr. Timothy Van Loon."

"Oh, Trix is hopelessly unworldly. The Van Loon connection does n't tempt her in the least. Timothy, as to whom, since they got him away from the ballet-girl he wanted to marry in Paris a year ago, his family have decided that he can't do better than take up with one of ours, is densely unconscious of the fact that Trix considers him a booby and a bore. However, we don't know what a year's apprenticeship to society may do for our débutante. She may wake up to her advantages in time."

"WHAT a very long name you have!"—Trix had progressed so far as to be saying to her neighbor, Mr. Brockenborough Vyvan, whose dinner-card her eye had lighted upon.

"Yes; our hostess has given me the full benefit of it. It was worse than that once. Reginald Alfred I was christened, after two uncles; but the fellows at college called me Brock, and when I came to New York to go into the offices of Clyde, Lawrence & Clyde,—they are building Mrs. Vernon's new house at Lenox, you know,—I cut loose from all the rest. I was sent by the firm once to wait upon a millionaire client, a rough old hay-seed, whom I found studying my card. 'Look a-here, young feller,' he remarked, by way of greeting, 'if you 're goin' to make your livin' out of us everage American citizens, take my advice and drop them tenderfoot frills off 'n your name. It 'll be worth many a dollar in your pocket, if you do.' And I did."

The girl's merry laugh rang out.

"Which was your university?" she asked, helping herself to something that tottered in a silver dish.

"Yale, of course," he answered, with proud promptitude.

"Why, it can't be you are—of course you are—Vyvan, '8–, the half-back that made the famous run at the Polo grounds, and won our game against Princeton!"

"Did you happen to be there?"

"I should say so! Jack and I were on top of a coach waving blue silk handkerchiefs; and I fairly shouted myself hoarse for you. To tell you the honest truth, when I saw you in that awfully dirty canvas jacket and trousers, chewing gum, just before you kicked the final goal, I thought I 'd rather know you than anybody in the world."

Vyvan tingled with satisfaction, to the ears.

"And who is Jack, if I may ask?"

"In the Yale catalogue, John Livingston Halliday, of the Freshman class—my brother, and the best friend I 've got."

"Yes, I know. He 's the fellow who brought to college from St. Peter's a reputation for rowing, and is talked of as likely to get a seat in the bow of this year's boat."

"I should say there is no doubt of that," said Beatrix, tossing her head complacently. "Jack captained the winning Matlock six last year. I wish you could see his arm muscle. It is very nice that he is pleased with Yale. He really likes it tremendously, I think."

"Does he?" said the amused alumnus.

"Oh, yes. He is pledged to 'Hay Boolay.'"

"Ah? That was my 'spot,' too."

"Was it? I 'm so glad. And I 'm hoping and praying Jack will get into Sk— What Senior Society were you in, Mr. Vyvan? Oh! *What* have I said? I *beg* your pardon," and, coloring with mortification at her heedless allusion to esoteric mysteries never to be uttered, she remained silent; nor was serenity restored until Vyvan led the talk into a discussion of the students' ball known as the Junior Promenade.

"She is as fresh as a daisy in the grass," reflected Brock. "I did n't believe it possible of a girl in society here. Queer thing she should have seen me make that run. But what have I to do with girls? It 'll be a long day before I can cast a second look at any of the little dears," ended this philosopher of twenty-four.

"Such delightful spirits has — I suppose I may say *our* little cousin Trix," murmured Mrs. Vernon, turning to Theobald. "I was remarking only yesterday to Mrs. Vane-Benson that all of the Halliday girls are so very different, and each so charming, so individual. People *will* ask me if Trix is going to marry Mr. Timothy Van Loon. I hardly think that fair to one of the family, do you?"

Mr. Theobald adjusted his monocle in his right eye, and looked at his hostess narrowly. He was a deliberate man, and her quick attack found him without a suitable reply. In his soul he was saying, "She is an amazing woman; and, upon my word, I believe she 'll win."

As for Cousin Tom, the old gentleman was already captive to the widow's wines and the excellence of her cookery. He did not know that her chef, who was a sympathetic soul as well as a master of the art of fencing, had composed the menu of this little entertainment under the title of a "Petit assaut d'armes." M. Alcide, with the rest of Mrs. Vernon's numerous retinue, perfectly understood the conditions of the case.

When they came out from dinner, the men to pass into a Pompeian smoking-room, their hostess brought her party to a halt in a little ante-chamber purposely left in shadow theretofore. There was a general exclamation of surprise. Facing each other on the wall-spaces, hung full-length portraits of Gerald and his mother, the frames sunk in maroon draperies that, lighted with electricity above, gave the startling effect of living presences in the group.

"Of course you recognize the artist?" said Mrs. Vernon, modestly. "They have but just come home from his atelier, and I could not deny myself the pleasure of seeing how they strike my guests."

"Strike me? They make me shiver," whispered Betty to Theobald. "If that man had painted Dr. Jekyll, people would have been sure to see in it the monster Hyde. They say he employs a little somebody with horns to come up through a trap-door and paint his eyes for him. The frankness of these is positively brutal."

The portrait of Mrs. Vernon represented that lady

standing in a gown of pinkish mauve satin, superbly rendered and full of glancing lights, against a background of azaleas of a purplish pink—a resplendent burst of color, and of an originality in technic that bespoke a master hand. But no one, brought face to face with it for the first time, could fail to perceive the fatal note of *bourgeoisie* it betrayed—the audacious revelation of untamed savagery beneath this wealth of flaunting beauty.

Gerald's portrait, on the other hand, was his living, breathing self, handsome and high-bred, with the dash of an hidalgo of old Spain. But Gerald's mother was not prepared for the effect it was to have on Trix.

"Oh! no, no!" cried the girl, putting her hands before her eyes. "That is not Jerry. It is somebody who has a cold heart, who is violent and self-willed, and would sacrifice any one he loves. I am sorry I looked at it, to have such a fancy get into my head."

"It is the old story," began Theobald, in the embarrassed silence produced by Trix's plain speaking. "Half the people one knows are at war with their portraits sent home from famous studios. In an age that has seen obloquy cast on an example of Meissonier—"

But Mrs. Vernon was not at once to be appeased by polite generalities. She was evidently ruffled, and in need of tangible consolation to recover her usual balance.

Fortunately, this was not long in coming to her. When they reached the opera-house, and settled with the fashionable swan-like pose into their chairs, Betty Halliday, who was in a line with Mrs. Vernon—Trix, rosy and brilliant, between the two—found herself in the box adjoining that of the social autocrat, Mrs. Van Shuter, known to the scoffers in the parquet as one of the "chatterboxes" in the parterre. Poor Mrs. Vernon, whose money had not yet purchased for her the right to disturb her neighbors with vapid conversation, had hitherto been obliged to remain in depressing silence through long evenings of metaphysics set to music. In despair she had secured a score, and tried to pose as a virtuosa in Wagner's music; but the effort proved too fatiguing, and she gave it up. Thus, she had returned to the privilege of studying every crease and surge of the fat Van Shuter back as it appeared overlapping a tightly laced corsage; the clasps of the various Van Shuter necklaces; the thin, flaxen Van Shuter hair, strained up over a pinkish cranium, and surmounted by plumes and jewels. All these were familiar spectacles, but she could not truthfully aver that she had seen the near front of the lady who sat through the opera-season like Buddha, vast, placid, twinkling with gems, satisfied to exist and to let herself be worshiped. During the weeks past, Mrs. Vernon had vicariously enjoyed reports, vouchsafed by Mrs. Van Shuter to her visitors, of Mrs. Van Shuter's attack of grippe, of Mr. Van Shuter's attack of grippe, and of the inroads of grippe on the constitution of Mrs. Van Shuter's confidential maid.

"'Dawson,' said I," had floated in from the great lady's box, "'if, when you first begin to sneeze, you will clap a porous plaster on your chest, grease your nose with mutton tallow, and take ten grains of quinine, you will certainly feel better the next day.' But Dawson was obstinate, and the result was what you know."

This much, even, had Mrs. Vernon been allowed to overhear—but alas! not as one privileged to sorrow with the sufferer. It would have been so sweet to breathe sympathy for Dawson into the ear of Dawson's mistress!

To-night, things were different. When Mrs. Vernon, wearing the renowned tiara, faultlessly gowned in modest pearl-color, appeared before the eyes of the multitude, leading old New York in chains, many observers took note of it, and resolved to leave on the morrow their tardy cards at Mrs. Vernon's door. Mrs. Floyd-Curtis, herself a lady recently promoted, mentally booked the widow for a dinner three weeks off. And, better than all, the ample bulk of the Idol turned slowly upon its satin-cushioned pivot, and Mrs. Van Shuter actually nodded and smiled toward Mrs. Vernon's box.

"You have not dined with me this year," she said to old Tom Halliday. To Theobald, over Betty's shoulder, "When are you coming to finish our nice talk about German baths? You are looking badly, and I wish you would try my little Doctor Bangs. He has done Mr. Van Shuter good, and he is doing Dawson good." Then to Betty, graciously, "You have heard from your sister? Florida, I am told. It was in Florida I caught the cold that lasted till after Easter of last year—in our own car, really. Who is the young man with Trix? Somebody brought him to my party before the last—yes, Vyvan, I remember; I shall have him

3

written in The Book, and—you may present Mrs. Vernon to me, if you like, my dear."

A few off-hand words from Betty, and the deed was done. Mrs. Van Shuter lifted her heavy eyelids, ducked her double chin; Mrs. Vernon's color rose, and her tiara tipped forward. Mrs. Vernon had crossed the Rubicon. Dick Henderson and Freddy de Witt rehearsed it afterward at the club, and a number of lorgnons took in the fact. But Mrs. Van Shuter's condescension did not stop at this.

"Your mother got the notice of the meeting at my house on Friday of next week?" she asked of Betty. "Tell her I count on her. There are so many coming who won't signify. It is to be a talk from that Mrs. Duncombe, the new woman who has had such success with the lower classes."

"What does she do to the lower classes?" Betty inquired.

"Oh! er—everything; it is a scheme for making working-women understand their legal rights against their husbands."

"I should think her chief trouble would be from the married couples between whom she interferes."

"Eh? oh! She says with a Fund an immense deal may be done. I made her understand that I can't be looked to to give money, with all I have to do. But I said they may meet first in my Empire room, and I let Miss Thompson write the notices."

"I suppose we shall know, when we get there, what it is all about," said Betty, fearlessly.

"Yes, certainly. There are to be flowers distributed among the poor, in pots—with little pamphlets revised

"MRS. VERNON HAD CROSSED THE RUBICON."

by lawyers. Perhaps Mrs.—ah—Vernon would like to come. If she would like to come, I don't mind telling Miss Thompson to write a card for her."

"She might; I don't know," said Betty. "She's awfully rich, and very generous. But I very much doubt her going unless you first call on her."

A surprised look made itself manifest upon the Idol's large pink face. But, then, everybody in town knows it was pains thrown away to be affronted by Betty Halliday.

"But you know, my dear, I never go in anywhere. And my first footman, James, engaged with me never to leave the box to ring a bell, except in an emergency."

"Tell James this is a very great emergency. I think, if you 're economically inclined, you 'll find it pay," said Betty Halliday, by whom it was pains thrown away to feel affronted.

"ELL," said Gerald, who was sitting by his wife on the veranda of a Florida hotel, "I never told you that, as we drove away from the house the day of the wedding to catch the Southern train — you know it had begun to rain — I saw Tony Theobald striding around the corner without an umbrella, and his face as black as thunder. Queer Dick, is Theobald. Don't suppose he 'd been having a row with anybody, do you?"

"Oh, impossible," said Nell.

She had her lap full of spring flowers, had been awakened by a mocking-bird trilling on the bough of an orange-tree that swept her window, was breathing softest air, looking under a blue Italian sky across the sparkling wavelets of a lovely lake. Gerald was at her side, heaven in her heart. She dismissed the subject of Theobald as she had all other clouds that drifted across the azure of her empyrean.

"Suppose we go out on the water," Gerald proposed after a lazy silence.

"Delicious. It is what I like best. Shall you row?"

"No; let 's have one of those black fellows,—one

38

who sings,—and loaf along till we feel like landing. What are you going in for?"

"To get parasol and gloves, of course. Anything you want?"

"Seems to me we might as well have left that pair of menials at home, for all the waiting on we get," said Gerald. "My man, when he's not smoking my cigarettes, is asleep; and your Swede sits reading Seaside Libraries when she is n't at her meals."

"Do you know, Gerald, there's something a little queer about that girl. She told me last night, when she was brushing out my hair, that she thinks Florida is stupid; that is to say, not stupid, but that there is a great deal of sand here, and the negroes and alligators are very much alike. Fancy finding Florida stupid!"

"Well, if the woman has nothing to do, and nobody to make love to her, perhaps the situation is different in her eyes. I'm afraid Hughes is a confirmed old bachelor; besides, he had a breach-of-promise suit in England once, and won't look at a woman since."

"Jerry, that reminds me, before I go—there's time enough, is n't there?"

"Bless you, yes. There's as much time as there is sand, in Florida."

"Now that you have spoken about your valet—I don't like to seem suspicious, but, really, there was rather a strange thing happened yesterday. You know, when the breeze fell, and you were kept out fishing with those men so much longer than you expected, I got a little nervous and fussy, and I went into your room and began turning over the things on your dressing-table. I found there the necktie I like so much,—the dark blue with the white speckles that you 'd taken off when you changed to flannels,—and, just to comfort myself a little, I—I—"

"Well—you—you—"

"I kissed it; and, happening to look in the glass, I saw behind me Hughes, who had come into the room in that noiseless way of his—"

"That 's his specialty; commands extra wages always. And Hughes did what?"

"Oh, he *did* nothing; but I caught an expression in his eye that I thought strange and sinister. When I turned around, rather sharply for me, he begged pardon, and did I know that the sail-boat was in sight? Of course this was a trifling circumstance, but I could not mistake that very peculiar look—"

"Nell, I 've a secret to tell you. You are a little gull. Hughes is the salt of the earth, as valets go; supports an old mother in England, and all that; and —now you 're going to be furious—I 've seen that expression on his face a thousand times,—it 's when he 's trying to *hold in a laugh!*"

"Jerry, I did n't think you could be so mean. If we 're to be spied upon, I wish we 'd left Hughes and Elsa in New York. Ever since old Norah had rheumatism I 've waited on myself; and I 'm always thinking how I should *love* to lay out your things for you."

"If you say so, I 'll send 'em both out in a leaky boat, and swamp them in the lake; though it would be easier to ship them home by train. Only, if we do, we 'll be guyed awfully. As you are passing the desk, ask if the post is in."

"O Jerry, we don't want any letters, and I have n't looked at a paper since the day after the wedding, when I saw those two nightmares purporting to be us, between a member of the rogues' gallery and somebody who makes three-dollar shoes."

"Well, they have done with us now. We are back numbers, and not wanted at any price. We may as well enjoy the woes of our successors. When I went to school in England a little American chap turned up who wrote to his governor in London: 'Dear Father: If you don't take me away, I 'll run away. Every fellow in the school has kicked me since I came!' At the end of a week he wrote again: 'Dear Father: I like it better than I did. A new fellow came to-day, and we 've all kicked him!'"

It was three weeks after the legitimate ending of the honeymoon, and they had been knocking around Florida, shunning the haunts of men and the beaten tracks of travel. For a time it had seemed as if they would need an eternity of isolation in which merely to discuss their reminiscences of meeting and falling in love. They took into the woods books and magazines, and read them upside down; invented childish devices to test and fathom their love for each other; spent hours in profound analyses and glorifications of each other, as to character and qualities. Gerald was astonished and, to his credit be it said, delighted with the crystal purity and grand directness of his wife's nature. He had never imagined a woman like her, and told himself that he would forever worship this Brunhilda as she deserved. And every day Eleanor's heart, shy and a little slow to expand in the new relation, grew to a broader understanding of and a greater reverence for the marriage bond. She thought of her mother's loss of a noble husband with new tears and with self-reproach that she had not bestowed on it enough of tender sympathy. Poor darling mama! To have had and lost, to have borne such anguish and survived it!

Eleanor's mind roved continually over the field of her acquaintance, trying to understand the apparent indifference to each other of most husbands and wives, the sharp words, the strained civilities, the perpetual friction upon minor points. She recalled how she had heard women fashion their own matrimonial differences into witty stories for the amusement of their listeners. How could it be that this had seemed to her merely a matter of poor taste; had repelled her only because of her constitutional reserve and horror of public comment? Now, it was as if a guardian of the holy of holies had seen some rude hand laid upon his treasure; she felt profaned, outraged, by the memory of things heard which she for the first time understood.

Jerry, who, we may be sure, received his full share of the outpourings of her heart upon these themes, was startled at her vehemence. The daily efflorescence of her beauty in her great love laid hold on and bewitched him utterly. Compared with the other women he had known, she was unique. Over and over again, when tempted to give some light answer to what he inwardly styled "her impossible theories," he was silenced by her lofty soul looking from its windows into his. He had a vague sense that he was ashamed to lay bare before such a gaze what his real man contained of unbelief and materialism on these points. And every now and again there crept into his mind a feeble wish that his wife would be a little less intense.

But she did not come back to him, after never so brief an absence, that his admiration was not stirred; and when she now returned, holding a sheaf of letters, and standing beside him to distribute them, the light touch of her garments thrilled him tenderly as he sat looking up into the morning freshness of her face.

"One from mama, one from Trix; all these for you, but only one that looks a bit interesting—a Florida postmark, a swell envelope, and crest. Why, Jerry, who has found us out?"

"It's a bore this getting letters, as you say," he answered, thrusting his batch into his breast-pocket, without noticing her question. "Shall I take yours too? Of course you've no pocket in that stunning tailor-made thing; but I forgive you, for it fits like a glove. Come, now, the day is well along."

Hughes rallied to the effort of spreading a rug in the bottom of the boat, and saw them off most affably —Nell, in her "tailor-made thing" of old-rose cloth picked out with silver, making, under her big hat, a picture her lazy lord was satisfied to scan to the exclusion of Floridian scenery. A handsome negro, like the Farnese Hercules in bronze,—who reminded them also of Tamagno in "Otello,"—his pink cotton shirt open to show his massive chest, his eyeballs and ivories flashing good-fellowship—handled the oars. Over a sheet of rippled blue, broken here and there by the snout of a traveling 'gator, and ringed with tropic foliage springing from golden sands, they dawdled idly, until the increasing vigor of the orb of day caused Jerry to break into irreverent quotation :

> The sun's perpendicular heat
> Illumines the depths of the sea,
> And the fishes beginning to —

"Not another word," said Nell. "You rob the hour of its sentiment. Let us go ashore at yonder point. I know a wood that is like the one wherein the poet dreamed of fair women ;

> "There is no motion in the dumb dead air,
> Nor any song of bird or sound of rill."

Their way led through the aisle of an orange-grove, its darkly shining leafage starred with white blossoms, and dotted with golden globes. Here and there a rain of Cherokee rose petals fell upon their path. An intoxicating fragrance filled the air to oppression, and clung to their hair and clothes. It was a relief to pass out into the dim wood beyond, and to rest on the grassless border of a still pool, as green as jade stone, an almost perfect circle, and exquisitely clear. Here, seated upon the rug, Jerry smoking a cigarette at her feet, Eleanor read her home letters, tasting them leisurely, and putting them back into their envelopes with a loving touch.

"Those dear people! How good and sweet they are, and yet, somehow, their letters seem to draw me back into that busy selfish world we have been trying to forget. Jerry, it is your turn now. Open your

budget, and while you are busy, I'll finish this story
I began nearly six weeks ago."

"I call it playing it pretty low down on an author
to take him along for honeymoon literature," Jerry
said, making no motion to obey.

"Read, Jerry dear; read your letters. Perhaps
there is something in them to entertain me with."

Gerald laughed a little constrainedly.

"The serpent has entered Eden. Confess, Nell, that
you are dying of curiosity about the one with a Florida postmark, in a man's hand that you don't recognize, bearing a crest you never saw."

"Coming so soon after that mysterious telegram
that Hughes brought you yesterday, that seemed to
worry you, and that you tore into little bits and
dropped into the lake—have n't I good right to be
suspicious?"

"Why, did n't I tell you?" he said, sitting upright
and speaking rapidly, while devoting himself to pick-
ing bits of moss and earth from his trousers. "That
telegram was from an old friend of mine who's down
here in his yacht—man I saw last, strangely enough,
when we parted at Tangier, where we'd come in with
a camel-train from Fez. You must do Tangier with
me next year, Nell, after we've finished Spain. Wonderful country Morocco is, though you'd no doubt
like Spain better—"

"And what is the old friend's name, Jerry, for I suppose he has one, although you neglect to mention it?"

"Best fellow in the world—not a lady's man exactly, and I'm not quite sure how you and he will hit
it off," he answered airily. "But he's the kind of

fellow I should n't like to offend — was married a year
or so ago to the surprise of all his friends, and they 're
down here at a bungalow he owns. The fact is, his
wife — well, I 'm not sure you and she would hit it
off," Jerry repeated flatly, and conscious of the same.

"Oh, you foolish boy, as if I don't see you are trying to hide something. Why on earth don't you tell
me who it is ? "

"This is his letter in my pocket. The letter said
the telegram would follow, — no, I mean the telegram
said the letter would follow, — so I was expecting it,
you see. His wife has egged him on, no doubt; they 're
dead set on getting us to visit them, and, hang me, if
I see how I can get out of it, considering I 'm under
tremendous obligations to Shafto in the past — "

"Shafto ? " said Eleanor, also sitting upright, a flush
coming into her face. "Not the man who married
that dreadful Mrs. King ? "

"Well, if it comes to that," answered Gerald, a little
resentful of her tone, "she was, when he married her,
in exactly the same position as Mrs. Clare and Mrs.
Lovell and Mrs. Luddington; all separated from their
husbands and married again with the sanction of holy
church. I don't claim that Mrs. Shafto is a nice woman
exactly, but the world has no right to accept the others
and taboo her."

"*That* Mrs. King ! " repeated Eleanor, with a cold
horror in her voice. "Why, when the papers were
filled every day with her divorce suit, my mother
burned them all, rather than let her children or servants come upon them. The worst of it was, Mrs.
King is a sort of relative or protégée of our old Aunt

Penfold, who refused to believe anything against her; but my mother got up once and left a room when Mrs. King came into it. Mama says she is an outrage on society."

Poor Nell, who had unconsciously committed the commonest error in tact of youthful wives, was quite taken aback by the vexed note, despite its attempt at pleasantry, of Gerald's answer:

"I should think a woman of the world would want to receive her ideas of such things from her husband, rather than hold on to the antiquated notions administered to her with schoolroom pap."

"Oh, but, Jerry dear," she persisted archly, "is n't it borne in on you by this time that I mean never to be a woman of the world?"

But Jerry refused to smile. It was not only that he felt strongly the usual objection of his sex to opposition in any form from hers; but the annoyance of Shafto's telegram had culminated in the receipt of this letter, about which he had foreseen that unpleasant complications were likely to ensue.

"All the same, Nell, your mother belongs to another world than yours and mine, now; and sooner or later you 'll come to recognize the fact. As long as I 'm with you, and sanction it, it can do no harm for you to mix a little with the friskies; and in a case like this it 's a good work disguised, you know."

He had suppressed his first flash of resentment, and Eleanor longed with all her heart to win back his smiles by acquiescence. But the stern stuff that had come down to her from a long line of Puritan ancestors would admit of no tampering with conscience.

"Jerry darling," she said pleadingly, "you know—I don't need to repeat it—that it would be a joy to me to please you in this thing; but, indeed, it would do no good; every instinct within me rebels against such society. It don't amuse me; and I'm no actor to cover what I feel. It isn't that I pretend to sit in judgment on them or any one. But, if you love me, don't spoil our life by bringing me into relations with that kind of people."

"'That kind of people!'" said her husband, angrily. "I wonder if it occurs to you that my habits are made, my friends chosen—that I can't throw over old chums because they're not up to the Halliday standard."

"Why, Jerry!" the girl said, in pained accents. So suddenly had their difference arisen, she could hardly believe her ears.

Gerald's eyes, fixed upon hers in displeasure, filled her with dismay. And, withal, she had the feeling one experiences in watching a pettish child in the process of "working himself up." The whole matter seemed too far beneath their love thus to imperil it. Denied the privilege of a weaker woman of melting easily—and, at this stage of married life, effectively—into tears, she sat in silence, while he strolled to some distance from the spot.

IV

O all appearance, Eleanor had hardly moved since Gerald left her, when he hurried back.

"I think you had better come now," he said in a constrained voice. "The wind is getting up, and it is no fun pulling across these lakes in the teeth of a blow."

They found the negro curled fast asleep in the boat hauled up on the beach, and, when aroused, he looked critically at the sky and water.

"I dunno, boss, how I kem to oversleep," he said. "Reckon 't was dancin' wid dem hotel gals at de breakdown till sun-up dis mornin'. I 'se jes got to row fer all I 'se wuth to git you an' de lady roun' dat p'int."

"We 're all right," Jerry answered, with new animation in his tone. Stripping off his flannel coat, loosening his shirt at the neck, and tossing aside his cap, he placed Nell in the stern of the boat, which the negro had run swiftly down the diamond sand into the water, and, when they took their places, possessed himself of a pair of oars, and the seat nearer his wife.

Without further warning the lake now whipped

4 49

itself into an angry sea. The cumbrous boat, laboring against a wind so chilled and fierce that it might have caressed an iceberg on the way, cut the waves briskly. Jerry, no longer the *fainéant* of the morning, alert, vigilant, prodigal of his great strength, his bare head rough, his brown cheeks reddened, his eye gleaming, moved his shoulders and steel-strung arms with the swing of a perfect machine. The negro, to whose experience hitherto it had not fallen to entertain the ex-stroke of a 'varsity crew unawares, gaped in open-mouthed admiration, trying to conform his slouching methods to Jerry's science. Eleanor, powdered with spray, disheveled by wind, huddled under her rug almost as excited as was the bow-oar. Sorrow banished, her heart swelled with pride in her gallant, beautiful young mate. No thought of danger assailed her with Jerry to the fore. She rejoiced in the mad bout against wind and waves. When, finally, they pulled in to the hotel-landing, and Jerry hoisted her upon the wharf from the little bobbing craft, she was too happy to notice at once the anxious faces gathered there, peering at a sail-boat far out upon the lake.

"It 's a boy, the son of the widow stopping at the hotel. She 's out driving, and knows nothing. All the other rowboats are away with a big party to Heron Bluffs. He 's a green hand, an' 'll swamp, sure as a gun."

These bits of information, afforded by one and another of the group of watchers, had but reached Eleanor's understanding, when she saw Gerald with a quick glance at the situation make ready to reëmbark.

"Who 'll come out with me—" Jerry had begun,

and the big boatman had answered, "I 'se yo' man, boss.   I 'se good fer it, if you is," when a flying form came down the path from the hotel.   It was the boy's mother, her face gray with terror, her lips hardly able to frame a question.   With instinctive tenderness, Eleanor put an arm around the poor creature's waist, and allowed the agonized face to hide itself upon her breast as the boat pushed off.

She got no good-by from her husband.   He was rowing for dear life, and yet it seemed intolerably slow progress to the lookers-on, who alternately watched his boat and the little reeling speck of white out on the yeasty water, under which they could plainly see a slight figure crouched against the mast.

It was over at last, the ordeal of waiting.   Eleanor, who had closed her eyes and tightened her clasp around the stranger in her arms, heard shout after shout from the watchers announce that the lad was saved.

"Here you are, youngster," Jerry said, later, thrusting the dripping boy into his mother's embrace. "None the worse for your little adventure, if I have n't made your head ache tugging at that tousled yellow mop.   For Heaven's sake, Nell, come along," he added, sotto voce, shaking himself like a water-dog to get rid at once of the wet, the pæans of lookers-on, and the hysterical blessings of the mother.   "All this fuss about a pull such as I have often taken on rough water and in greater danger; it was nothing.   But we timed it well, I must say, for the kid's boat capsized just as we reached the spot."

Nevertheless, when they were alone in their own room, Eleanor, who had kept down her feelings, cast herself with sudden fervor upon her husband's neck.

"Hullo!" said Jerry, good-humoredly.

"Oh, my own glorious darling!" she cried. "How could there have been a shadow between our hearts? Jerry, I don't believe I ever knew what love is, till now!"

V

"I DON'T mind telling you, Nell," Gerald said the day following his adventure in the boat, "that Shafto, who is the most generous fellow living, came to my aid once when I was in the biggest kind of a scrape in Paris—hauled me out of it, set me on my feet, saved me from having to appeal to my mother, who was already cutting up pretty rough about my extravagance, et cetera. Would n't take thanks, much less money—though I 've squared that since—bound me over never to mention his name in the affair. And how was I to say a downright no to anything *he* asked me—"

"Don't speak of it, dearest," she cried, growing pale at the memory of their brief estrangement. "It 's I who was silly not to divine. What does anything matter if we love and understand each other? There, give me his note again. On Thursday, by the 11.30 train to Badajoz, he says, to stay till Monday afternoon. Jerry, it 's all settled, of course, dear. As you say, we must make the best of it; but don't you think she—they—would be satisfied if we left them on *Saturday?*"

4*   53

"Easy enough to manage that when we get there," answered Jerry, in high good humor. "You brave creature, you look like the leader of a forlorn hope."

"Oh, if you only knew," she said, leaning down to rest her cheek on his, in the great need of love that was to this woman, as to all women, the impulse over-powering judgment, "how wickedly happy I am in doing what pleases you!"

"You're a greenhorn to show your cards thus early in the game," he answered, feeling convinced, however, that she was really a sage. "And about this visit to the Shaftos bothering you, it really need n't be such a bugbear if you go in for it pluckily. It may end in quite a lark for you; who knows?"

Eleanor, in spite of her heroism, shivered a little here.

"Oh, no, no; I'm rather a coward, Jerry, for all I look so brave. For Major Shafto's sake,—he must be a noble if mistaken man,—let us try to be resigned. It will be a bore to you, Jerry; I'm sorry to think of that. They have friends stopping there, he says—a small house-party. Now, who can her friends be?"

"Your mother's Aunt Penfold, perhaps," suggested Jerry, with malice prepense.

"You wretched boy, how dare you? Aunt Penfold is her godmother, I think, and there has always been a dread in the family lest the old lady, who is what Betty calls pig-headed, should leave all her money to Sophy King—Shafto, I mean. I saw her at Aunt Penfold's in my school-girl days—a showy creature with black hair and snapping black eyes. I was wild with ambition to dress like her, I remember."

"Her hair's red now,—or blonded, as I believe you women say,—and she's a bouncer in size and style. I believe in my soul that Shafto married her because he thought he'd stand by her before the world. He's an awful flat where women are concerned; but he's only to see you, to know you're of a different sort, and he won't push the thing again. And she—why, you'll no móre mix than oil and water; she'll be wanting to get rid of you instead of holding on. Don't bother your head about that, my pretty Puritan."

"But I can't help wondering why, when she knows what mama has always thought of her, she should want to get me to be her guest. O Jerry, you men are bigger and broader than we! Here am I, doubting and suspecting, and you, having made up your mind to do a generous thing, never change or falter, but go straight ahead, almost as if you like the idea of going to that racketing woman's house."

"I forgot to say," he answered, waiving discussion on the last suggested point, "you may as well prepare yourself. I'll bet ten to one Kitty Foote will be one of their party."

"Kitty Foote?" echoed Eleanor, faintly.

"She was traveling bridesmaid, or what do you call it, on their late trip to Alaska, and she and Sophy Shafto are as thick as thieves just now. Of course that horsey, doggy kind of girl isn't to your taste, but, at least, she's accepted everywhere. The Van Loons had her at Newport stopping with them last year, and she goes into the best houses. I think that kind of boy in petticoats is a first-class bore, myself;

and most men agree with me. They call her 'good old Kitty,' at the clubs. She is n't clever, she 's as ugly as a mud-fence, and her people are of no consequence; but she 's invited more than any girl I know, simply because she 's a social stop-gap, and always can be had."

"Is n't she the intimate friend of your friend Hildegarde de Lancey?" asked Eleanor.

"I 've met her there," Jerry answered. "Look below, at this funny old darky, Nell, trying to get his mule past the gate-post with a load of garden stuff. He is remonstrating with the beast as if it were a brother or a son."

The side window of their sitting-room looked down upon a service road, leading between dwarf-oranges and palmettos to the rear of the hotel. There was no one in sight, and the voice of the gentle old negro, his skin, hair, beard, and clothing alike as gray as the hanging-moss of his native woods, was heard, unconscious of observation, in soft rebuke.

"Hi, muel! What you doin' dar, muel? I done told you 'bout dat ar pos' day befo' yistiddy."

"O Jerry dear, to think of leaving this Arcadian place!" said Nell, as the listeners laughed together. "I shall always remember it as heaven on earth."

"If monotony 's your standard—" began he.

"Hush! I forbid you," she said, putting her hand over his mouth.

"For a man who is not running a railway, or booming land, or growing oranges, or—spooning—" he succeeded in getting out.

"Jerry!"

"The uses of rural Florida may *be*—but—"

"Oh, please don't, dearest! What you are going to say will give me a real pang. I don't know how it is, but I am getting to be afraid to let you know how much I think of—things," she concluded irrelevantly.

"I know enough to be convinced that you are what my mother's chef said of a salad of lettuce sprinkled with fresh violets and old Bordeaux he sent up recently—'*vraiment lyrique.*' There, let's kiss and be friends, and forgive me for teasing you."

She stood a while with his arm around her waist, looking out in the fullness of contentment at the dancing waters of the lake under the white and green and gold of an arch of orange-boughs.

"Only two days more of this, and then to the busy world again," she murmured. "Who would believe there is an actual New York? How still it is to-day! One could almost hear a pin drop."

"No such good luck as to hear a pin drop," Jerry laughed, taking out his watch, and discovering with animation that he had just time to walk to the railway station for the daily excitement of seeing the northern train halt on its southward way.

THERE was nothing lyrical in the next appearance before the callous outside world of Mr. and Mrs. Gerald Vernon. They went down to Badajoz on the 11.30 train on Thursday, like any other pair of smart tourists, in a compartment to themselves, with the valet and maid in seats just outside of it, those two long-suffering underlings having the appearance of subdued rejoicing at a move in no matter what direction.

The usual paraphernalia of silver-mounted traveling-bags, rugs as soft as down, umbrellas, sticks, and parasols strapped together into an obese roll, top-coats, and English waterproofs, littered their sofa and filled their racks. The great bunch of violets that Gerald had ordered to follow his wife during every day of her absence from New York scattered its sweetness from the breast of Eleanor's jacket. The young couple bore every mark of prosperous conventionality. Nell, who in her secret soul would have preferred, at that moment, to be sitting alone with Gerald on a desert island, as Paul and Virginia are pictorially seen, under the shelter of a single palm-leaf, could not understand the rather exhilarated manner with which her husband went off for a visit to the smoking-car, "just to see if any one he knew was on the train." It did not occur to her that Jerry, manlike, now that he knew their dawdling time was over, rejoiced in their swift rush onward, keenly relished contact with his kind, and found new satisfaction in railway sights and sounds. During their short expedition, he was liberal to the porter to the extent of filling that sated soul with gratitude, burdened Hughes and Elsa with "all the latest novels and magazines," and, for one brief moment, even felt a pang of regret that he could not bring himself to make a purchase from the peddler of travelers' caps.

Badajoz, where the train, speeding on, left them under the Queen Anne roof of a pretty little station, was one of the speculative products of modern Florida,—a brand-new town, built on the edge of a little sapphire lake where herons stalked, surrounded by woods full of red-bud, with yellow jasmine garlanding the trees, and all manner of sweet wild flowers sharing an undergrowth with moccasins and black-snakes and other reminders of a subtropical region. Streets and town-lots, big with intention, were staked off on all sides, but of actual village there was little, and what there was bore the appearance of having been taken out of packing-boxes, newly painted and varnished, and set up over-night. Hidden by the station, Major Shafto's dog-cart was in waiting, the Major himself occupied with soothing a pair of fretting bays. He was a bluff, bearded man, of a matter-of-fact demeanor, and as Eleanor accepted the seat beside him, Jerry perching behind, and the servants following in a trap with the grooms and luggage, she could hardly believe that this commonplace personage was the hero of a marriage as recklessly chivalric as that of any figure in romance. While the horses, released from durance and suspicion of the engine, shot forward on a sandy road through the gloom of a pine-wood, she ventured a glance sidewise at her charioteer, half expecting, as Jerry afterward declared, "some development of the bucaneer variety." It was almost a disappointment that, what between her husband and the horses, their host found time to bestow on her only a few of those meager conventional civilities that make a woman feel her presence thrown away. It was when they turned in at an avenue hedged with oleander and twinkling laurel that the first surprise was accorded her.

"As I wrote you, there are people stopping here," Major Shafto said indifferently. "Friends of my wife's, you know. Man you 've met perhaps, Vernon, —Lord knows what women like in him,—that English fellow, Carteret Leeds; then, Miss Foote and her brother, and Mrs. de Lancey, that Mrs. Shafto wired to come down from the Ponce de Leon; and—so, Beauty; quiet, Booty, you brute—I believe young Van Loon is due to-night."

"Timothy?" began Jerry, with a whistle, but the horses, shying at a watering-pot supplementing a wheelbarrow near the drive, obviated the necessity of a reply. He was on the ground to help his wife when they pulled up at the door.

An ideal retreat for Loves and Graces was the Bungalow, massed in verdurous shrubbery, its slanting roof and verandas overrun with Cherokee roses, between tall palmetto-trees, under a sky of intense blue —sufficiently far from the madding crowd of Florida tourists, and yet near enough for convenience; like the "desert" of Lady Juliana, the spoiled London beauty in Miss Ferrier's delightful old novel, "a beautiful place, all roses and myrtles, not absolutely out of the world, where one can give fêtes champêtres and déjeuners to one's friends."

It was a marvel to see how the ambulating proprietors, who had come south in their yacht not a fortnight before, had contrived to give the Bungalow an air of luxurious finish, as if they had lived there since the planting of the first vine. The broad veranda, spread with rugs, had the customary array of little tables containing brass pots of growing plants, reviews, magazines, and paper-knives, drawn up at the elbows of wicker chairs, under hanging lamps set

"AWFULLY KIND OF YOU TO COME TO OUR LITTLE SHANTY IN THE WILDERNESS."

with bosses of colored glass, and much ironmongery in spirals and curlicues. There was a hammock of yellow-and-white netting, dangling with tassels like the mount of a Spanish muleteer; and this was filled with cushions of silk in rainbow hues. There were screens and sofas, porcelain garden-seats, a medley of the picturesque effects with which we are all familiar nowadays. From somewhere at the rear of the house arose the sound of voices over a game of tennis, and, issuing from a hall crowded with Japanese curios, appeared a smug butler attended by a fresh-faced young underling in maroon livery with a striped waistcoat, both of whom might have just emerged from a class-meeting, so guileless did they appear. Eleanor, whose heart had begun to beat at the nearness of the dreaded encounter, was relieved by these every-day apparitions; nor was she further alarmed upon the arrival from the tennis-ground of their hostess, holding over her bare head a large white lace parasol, and letting float behind her a graceful trail of crinkled stuff cleverly adjusted to conceal the tendency to flesh that afforded her continual concern. Mrs. Shafto came toward them swiftly, a little nervously, but carrying it off with a fine show of hearty welcome, and talking to preclude the possibility of answer.

"Awfully kind of you to come to our little shanty in the wilderness," she said to Eleanor when the first bustle of arrival lulled. "I told Shafto I thought you might like to bring Mr. Vernon to visit so old a friend. I won't claim acquaintance for myself, though I saw you as a school-girl at your Aunt Penfold's long ago."

"I remember perfectly," Eleanor answered, blushing, and looking about her. "What a pretty place you have! This is not my idea of the wilderness at all."

"The modern conception of roughing it," chimed in Jerry, who had kept close to his wife's elbow.

"Oh, it was easy enough. We sent a lot of people down before us, and they did it all," said Mrs. Shafto, superbly. "Come in and see our 'living-room,' as we call it. I made Lebel get this glazed chintz with the big gillyflowers from Paris, and he sent a Frenchman to drape the walls and curtains. The rest is, as you see, principally Florentine mirrors and brocade photograph-frames, and a lot of easy-chairs and couches. What shall they fetch you — shandygaff, or lemon-squash, or a B. & S., till luncheon-time? When you're ready, we can go out on the tennis-court a bit."

"Shafto tells me you've got a houseful," Jerry said, over his shoulder, as he bent down to look at a glass case of miniatures.

"Yes; we brought all but Hilda in the yacht. She was at the Ponce de Leon nursing a wretched cold, and we wired at once for her, poor dear, and she came over with Miss Shaw."

"Miss Shaw?" asked Jerry, as they set out to stroll around the house and through the grounds.

"Yes; her companion, the sheep-faced old thing who used to knit in corners — don't you remember? Began as governess to the little girls, who are with Hilda's mother, now. Well, she's here, and Kitty and Leeds do nothing but run rigs on her, and she never finds it out. Did Shafto tell you we're to have Timothy to-night?"

"I heard he is in these parts under the delusion he is trying for tarpon."

"That's a new name for it," said Mrs. Shafto, shooting at him a gleam from her eye. "You *have* been out of the world not to know that since your young sister-in-law turned the cold shoulder upon the heir of the Van Loons, he has developed another flame."

"Confound him for a jackanapes!" said Jerry, flushing a little. "The fellow's always getting into messes with feminines. I wonder his dear mama don't send a nursery-maid along to keep him from making acquaintance with strange little girls."

They had fallen behind Major Shafto and Eleanor, and she dropped her voice.

"Oh, but you are the one to make allowances in this case. A year ago you might have even sympathized—she has quite turned his brain."

"His *what?*" growled Jerry, blackly.

"Oh, well, what passes for that organ in his anatomy. He is fairly infatuated, and would marry her to-morrow if—"

"If what?"

"If he were not chiefly dependent on his affectionate parents, who are nothing if not respectable, and couldn't stand a blot in the Van Loon escutcheon. That's not such an out-of-the-way, unheard-of condition of affairs, eh? It seems to me I was the confidante, a year ago, of a greatly superior young man, in very much the same predicament."

"For Heaven's sake, take care," he said hurriedly.

"Don't be afraid. I am discretion itself. Even Shafto don't know how near you came to—but the

5

best of the joke about Timothy is that Hilda has ceased to laugh at him. That is always dangerous, I've found. You know he inherited from an old aunt a year or two ago, and there's enough cash for them to wait on till the family comes around—"

"Look here," he said bruskly, as they turned the corner of the house where Shafto had stopped to point out to Eleanor his pet grove of oranges. "I thought I knew you pretty well, but I'll be hanged if I understand what you brought us here for."

"It was Major Shafto, who quite longed to see his dear old friend," she answered demurely. "How could I suppose you'd be getting excited over Hilda's affairs of the heart, now you are a married man? Pray calm down. I know those sudden tempests of yours, and how hard you used to find it to hold them in when you and I and Hilda were at Sioux Falls last year. But I could n't have expected to see one *now*, could I?"

"I wish I had n't let you worm my folly out of me that time," he said bitterly. "Though you pretended to stand my friend in the matter, it is certain you never did me any good."

"Oh, come, come!" she said chidingly. "It is your mother who should be charged with all the blame of interference and disaster. But what does it matter now? This is a poor time to quarrel. You must behave yourself, and help me to make it pleasant for —we must all be on our good behavior—your beautiful young wife."

"One word only," he said. "I would have written this beforehand, but I thought I could trust it to your

good nature. Eleanor knows nothing of that affair.
You will let—sleeping dogs lie?"

"Of course. What possible motive could I have to
do otherwise? We are talking of Major Shafto's dogs,
Mrs. Vernon," she said smoothly, as the others came
up with them. "You must make him take you to his
kennels. Our man has had such wonderful luck this
year with dachshunds — Yes; that tree covered with
yellow jasmine is pretty, is n't it? Here we are. You
know every one, I believe? I really think myself
very clever to get up such a meeting of old friends."

Gerald had run upon the Shaftos the year before,
when they had gone West to be rid of the odium of
newspaper comment upon their marriage, and, presented by the Major to his wife, had been speedily
established as a confidential friend of the menage. In
his then frame of mind it had been an immense comfort to tell somebody—and especially a nice, jolly,
kind-hearted woman who had herself felt the world's
rubs, and could sympathize—about his mad passion
for that loveliest and most ill-used of creatures, Hildegarde Smithson, then a resident of Dakota, awaiting
her freedom from a hateful bond. Finding such con-
genial society, Mrs. Shafto persuaded her Major to
stay his steps in Sioux Falls for a while, and the four
had spent their days together in riding and driving
and such other amusements as the place afforded.
Under these circumstances, it was not long before
Mrs. Shafto became possessed of the secret aspiration
of Jerry's heart—to marry Hildegarde as soon as the
law should set its fairest victim free. Now, as the
canons of modern story-writing allow no suggestion

of a mystery in the story's plot, we may make haste
to say that this discovery did not please Mrs. Shafto
in the least.   She was jealous and mischievous, and,
like the Grim Reaper, wanted all men for her harvest.
Her first move was to let her Hercules-in-toils, the big
Major, who was ignorant of women's wiles, go off on
a hunting expedition, taking Jerry with him, in search
of deer and bear, which at most times will comfort
man for the absence of his feminine enslaver.   When
they returned, and Gerald flew to the presence of Mrs.
Smithson, he was encountered on the way by an imperative telegram from his mother in New York, bid-
ding him come home in the interests of important
business.   And when he had at once packed his portmanteau, and started for home, Mrs. Shafto, in the
most complacent manner in the world, rubbed her
hands as if to be rid of a tiresome episode, and in-
formed the Major that it was time to set forth upon
their still farther western journey.   Before leaving,
she breathed a tender adieu to her charming Hildegarde, who, whatever she felt, was in no position to
give token of discomfiture.

When the triumphantly liberated Mrs. de Lancey,
late Smithson, again encountered Gerald Vernon, in
Lenox, six months later, he was in the train of a girl
who, everybody said, would marry him if he really
meant business.   Gerald had meant business, had
married Eleanor Halliday, and had compromised with
his conscience about forsaking Hildegarde by induc-
ing his mother-in-law to send her an invitation to the
wedding.

Now, when they met at the Bungalow, he sat quite

content on a little iron bench beside her, talking com-
monplaces, and watching Kitty Foote jump about,
performing prodigies of tennis in a match of singles
with Mr. Carteret Leeds.   Spite of his little spasm of
resentment of the enamored Timothy, Gerald looked
from Hilda over at his blooming, innocent Nell, and
asked himself if it were just a year ago that he had
gone off from Sioux Falls ready to blow his brains
out for the sake of this woman, whose face looked a
little worn in the full light of day.   He was even
critical about the lines of Hildegarde's figure, hitherto
esteemed peerless, and decided that it did not compare
with that of his young Diana, tall and slim and long-
waisted, her head so grandly set upon her long, full
throat.   And when he asked Mrs. de Lancey as to
the health of her two little darlings,—"so pretty and
quaint with their hair like spun silk,"—he felt a sense
of devout gratitude that he was not at the moment
sharing, as it were, the paternal rights over these
blessings with the very objectionable Smithson, who
was still living in the family mansion, and conducting
business in his usual place in New York, and was lia-
ble to be met in the usual haunts and thoroughfares.
He recalled with forgiveness the tremendous outburst
of temper with which his mother had favored him
when he acknowledged to her charge his intention to
wed Mrs. Smithson.   He had long ceased to smart
over the convincing argument—a threat of utter
disinheritance—by which his mother had conquered
him.   And he never once suspected whose had been
the hand that had set the machinery in motion to
alter the current of his life.   Altogether, he was

5*

proud to have stood the test of meeting Hilda so suc-
cessfully.

By dinner-time Nell had begun to feel more at ease
in what her mother would have called this dubious
house. So long as nothing appeared to shock the eye
and sense, there was even something rather fascinating in her feeling of independence as a young wife,
with no one to account to but a facile, smiling husband, who made light of so many of her inherited
prejudices. Mrs. Shafto, brusk and jovial, amused
her. She liked the Major, and Mrs. de Lancey was
one of those women whom all women admire and pet.
Even the tomboy Kitty Foote showed to better advantage in a bungalow than at the gatherings of conventionality in town. But Eleanor could not be lenient
to Mr. Carteret Leeds.

He was an Englishman who had been wafted on
his way into American society by favoring gales. Five
or six leading families, like Homer's cities for Homer
dead, disputed for him the first winter he appeared;
but when interrogated, no member of any family
could say who had discovered or introduced him. For
a while inquiry had been appeased by a rumor that he
was a younger son of Lord Kirkstall, come to New
York to go into trade; but to a visiting American
his lordship had indignantly disclaimed any offshoot
whatever in America, adding incidentally, that he
did n't think one of his sons would fancy living in
the States, where it must be so uncommonly nasty to
be served only by blacks, you know. The disclaimer
being duly reported, upon the visiting American's return, found Mr. Carteret Leeds in full swing at New-

port, where he was of too decided a social value to be lightly cast away. He was an authority on polo and cricket, on horse-play in English country houses, and in the hunting-field, and no one liked to think of the void his absence would create; so it was decided to ask no more questions, but to accept this nice, mysterious man without home or friends or country. Still, ignorant people would occasionally err, and Leeds was once put upon a committee of arrangement to draw up a schedule of unprecedented gaieties in honor of an English prince who never came; this honor, however, he declined without explanation of any kind— which, in the opinion of some conservatives, was the best evidence of sense Mr. Leeds had yet afforded.

Mrs. Halliday's home in New York had been one of those that had not opened its portals to Mr. Leeds, and Eleanor disliked extremely being thrown in the intimacy of a house-party with a person who was more than suspected of using his social opportunities to furnish personalities at so much per column to journals of the baser sort. So she greeted him with bare civility, and, in response to a venture upon his part congratulating her upon "leavin' the fossils," and "comin' in with the knowin' set," straightened her back and stared at him with such cold surprise that for once Leeds was subdued, and reckless Mrs. Gerald had an enemy the more written upon her list.

Little Foote, Kitty's brother, a shadowy presentment of his own idea of a "swagger" Englishman, was more amusing than injurious to society. His innocent pleasure was to be forever changing clothes that he had lately bought in London. He was volu-

ble in lisping about the movements of the fashionable
world, in a curious dialect compounded of American-
ese and Mayfair English. And he looked up to Mr.
Carteret Leeds as to a Mentor whom it were pride to
heed.

Dinner brought with it Mr. Timothy Van Loon, of
whom it cannot be said that his distinguished position
in the American aristocracy was manifest in his appearance. He was tall and thin, with pale hair and
pinkish eyelids, and a feathery, pale mustache. At
his coming, the matrons and maids of society were so
wont to melt into exceeding friendliness, so accustomed was he to see men of mature age, of distinguished achievement, of personal attraction, forsaken
at his approach, that in his own infallibility to please
he had come to put a trust no circumstance could
shake. As to him was allotted the hostess to take in,
and Eleanor sat upon the Major's right, Gerald and
Mrs. de Lancey were partners during the dinner hour,
and it was plain to behold the discomfort poor Timothy endured. He grew sullen, drank freely, left his
hostess to sustain a monologue; and Eleanor, seeing
her husband for the first time bestowing on another
woman the attention that had been hers exclusively,
sighed while chiding herself for a weakness she con-
temned. She resolved to make up for this her unconscious cerebration by an especial overture of friendliness to Mrs. de Lancey when the women should meet
after dinner in the drawing-room.

The evening, like the day, passed without incident.
The absent spirit of Mrs. Halliday might have been
placated by its restraint. "It was so deadly dull,"

Mrs. Shafto told Leeds in the smoking-room afterward, "we thought of asking some one to recite." When the ladies assembled in the hall to take their bedroom candlesticks, Gerald spoke for a moment to his wife.

"I shall be late, probably," he said; "we've a game of cards on, and you must n't keep awake."

While Mrs. Vernon's maid was still brushing her brown hair, and Eleanor, her eyes fixed upon the floor, was deciding that she should certainly hold to her first plan of leaving the Bungalow on Saturday, female forms clad in trailing tea-gowns were stealing past her door, and flitting down the stairs. A little later, when Elsa had been dismissed, Eleanor heard strange sounds from the bowling-alley near the house —music, dancing, and shrieks of hilarious laughter that were not all from the ruder sex. Feeling uncomfortable, the young wife stole out into the corridor with a vague hope of summoning her husband to her side. There, hovering over the banister, in a frilled short-gown and petticoat, she encountered the spectral figure of Miss Shaw, who was bathed in tears.

"Oh, my dear, this is too much!" moaned the ancient maiden, wringing her hands. "It's bad enough to see ladies smoking cigarettes and playing cards till all hours every night; but here they have got up a sort of fancy ball in the bowling-alley, and—I 'm ashamed to tell you—that Mr. Leeds has gone and got on my —my night-things over his dress-suit, and has been dancing a skirt-dance with Miss Foote in her brother's clothes."

"I must see my husband," said Eleanor, hotly.

"This must be stopped—Jerry will stop it *at once;* there is *nothing* so despicable to him!"

But, alas! at this moment, full in their sight, Jerry, wearing a fool's costume and bells, with a lighted cigar between his teeth, pranced through the hall below, followed by the untiring Kitty Foote attired as Columbine, and Mr. Timothy Van Loon as Harlequin, all three evidently on their way to appear in a new variety of entertainment before the audience awaiting them in the impromptu theater.

Poor Eleanor, too proud to mingle her tears with those of the disconsolate Miss Shaw, ran back to her room, and cried herself to sleep.

VI

T was clear to the widow Vernon's critics that a sweet little cherub of some kind was sitting up aloft keeping watch over her social progress —she was so plainly and provokingly on the rise. Mrs. Peter Van Shuter, having convinced her James that the occasion justified the effort, that stately one, his scorn ill concealed by the collar of a large fur cape, alighting at a convenient hour from the box of the well-known blue chariot bearing the Van Shuter crest, delivered into the hands of Mrs. Vernon's menial at her front door a couple of visiting-cards. One of these bits of pasteboard revealed "Mrs. Van Shuter" simply; her residence was supposed to be known to all the initiated—for the vulgar herd it had no possible concern. The smaller card, representing the Idol's humdrum little spouse, had to the larger the same relation in size and modest bearing sustained by Mr. Van Shuter to his lady in the flesh.

When James had performed his duty, and received an apologetic "To the park" from his mistress's lips, the carriage drove away, but not before Mrs. Vernon, —whose victoria awaited her descent, her footman,

the double of Mrs. Van Shuter's, remaining in a statu-
esque pose upon the curbstone,—happening to glance
through the silk curtains of her morning-room, had
the advantage of seeing Mrs. Van Shuter's knees. She
recognized the carriage and liveries, and felt, in the
impatient drawing up of the rug over an ample lap,
that if knees could speak, those said, "Now I have
done it, let me go." Mrs. Vernon, however, went on
buttoning her gloves quietly, and, when the cards were
handed in, glanced at them with admirable self-control.
But as she leaned back in the victoria, and allowed herself, also, to be driven to the park, a smile relaxed her
visage into satisfaction no longer to be restrained.

Lent was under way, and among the penitential
exercises in order for the fashionable world was the
meeting at Mrs. Van Shuter's, to be conducted by the
most recent society fad, a Mrs. Calliope Duncombe,
who had suddenly appeared as a herald of a woman's
movement in behalf of fellow-women—whence, nobody knew.

As everybody is aware, a women's meeting of this
class means the collection of a fund, and as collecting
a fund entails more or less ordering around of other
people, distribution of patronage, and seeing one's
name in print, it is always popular. Add to this that
the affair was to be nurtured and coaxed into promi-
nence in the cream-and-gold Empire salon of Mrs.
Peter Van Shuter, and there was small doubt of its
vogue.

Mrs. Vernon, thanks to Mrs. Van Shuter's two bits
of pasteboard, now saw no reason why she might not
go to this convocation with self-respect. But she

THE MEETING IN MRS. VAN SITTER'S EMPIRE ROOM.

resolved so to dress and demean herself, and so to time her arrival, that the fact of her presence should bring all it was worth.

At eleven A. M. on the appointed day, the handsome room, with its walls hung in pumpkin-colored damask between panels of ivory and gilt, its crystal chandeliers and cabinets of curios, was filled with ladies seated upon spindling gilt chairs. Assembled there with an honest intention of making money for a fund, most of them had entered no farther into an understanding of the affair than that Mrs. Van Shuter's Miss Thompson had addressed the invitations for them to meet in Mrs. Van Shuter's famous Empire room. Pending the opening of the proceedings, a chatter went on, gaining strength till it reached the ear-piercing climax known among congregations of our American fair. Voices strained to shrillness met and clashed in the air. They talked of—bodily complaints, table-waters, faith-cure; the excellence of rival schools as illustrated by their respective progeny; one's anxiety in bringing out a girl; the rudeness of young men one takes the trouble to invite; the butler's asthma and the chef's impertinence; their recent travels, to which nobody would listen because every one had traveled recently; the latest scandal— one of the current week, since all earlier were forgotten; spring plans, summer plans; the name and author of the naughty novel nobody must read; and the fact that the last diamond necklace of one of their leaders had cost fifty thousand dollars more than that belonging to her sister-in-law, who had gone into mortified retreat.

Mrs. Van Shuter, august and sleepy, sat by a table at the far end of the room — around her two or three of those ladies, important as ball-and-dinner-givers, who are rightly reckoned our true nobility. In the lap of this grandeur, a meek-looking woman in a Quakerish bonnet and plain brown gown remained with down-dropped eyes, awaiting her signal to arise.

"Dear me! It is half-past! Are n't they ready to begin?" said Mrs. Bullion to Mrs. Van Shuter.

"I hope so," said Mrs. Van Shuter, yawning. "If they don't, it will make us late for lunch, and I can't be made late for lunch."

"Then you must call the meeting to order," said Mrs. Bullion, briskly. She was president of a Baby Hospital, and knew her business well.

Thus prodded, Mrs. Van Shuter wearily took up a paper-knife inlaid with turquoise and coral, and knocked with it on a table of buhl and malachite. She had only one fear—that it might be voted to raise the fund by subscription, and that she would have to head the list. In the hush that ensued, several unconscious women on the outskirts went on talking to one another as before.

"If *my* husband had that cough, I 'd put him in flannel from top to toe," remarked one lady at the highest pitch of her voice; then, covered with confusion, she sank into obscurity.

Next, Mrs. Calliope Duncombe, having been preluded and introduced, stood upon her feet, with a deprecating smile, while her patronesses wrangled over some point of parliamentary law. At this precise moment Mrs. Vernon, last to arrive, was ushered by a footman

between the folds of a yellow satin door-curtain at the
lower end of the room, and remained standing long
enough for every one present to be aware of her iden-
tity. Then with a little bend of the head in the direction of the hostess, and nods here and there about the
crowd, she sank leisurely into a chair, let fall away
from her a cloak rigid with Russian sables, crossed
her gloved hands lightly upon her lap, and prepared
to listen.

It was undoubtedly a well-managed entrance, that
struck conviction home to many souls. But the keen
eyes of Betty Halliday, perhaps the most interested
person in the throng, saw a change coming over Mrs.
Vernon's face as her gaze rested upon the speaker of
the day. She flushed, withdrew a little into the shade
of the curtain, fidgeted, lost her imperial calm. Curious Betty looked from her again to the lecturer, but
in the mild visage under the poke-bonnet discovered
nothing. In a musical voice, with a pleading manner,
Mrs. Duncombe began her smooth appeal.

With her argument, this narrative has no desire to
deal. From her opening statement, that history everywhere has shown that, in proportion as women have
had the right to protect themselves, they have freed
themselves from inglorious burdens, to the closing
reminder, that it is woman's place to bear good tidings
of release to her suffering sisters, Betty, and unbe-
lievers like her, felt a strange desire to laugh. They
could not, however, deny to Mrs. Duncombe the possession of that magnetic eloquence of manner that
often clothes weak speech with power to move an
audience. Many of her hearers wiped their eyes,

6

some took notes upon tablets hanging at their chate-
laines. Every woman who took notes did so with an
intention of bringing Mrs. Duncombe's schemes for
resistance to arbitrary man to bear upon her own
domestic lawgiver, and was afraid she would not remember to quote them exactly right. For there was
this inevitable feature of some women's acceptance
of new doctrine—each one instinctively tested every
plea, argument, or illustration advanced by the speaker, upon her own relations to the husband of her
choice.

Betty, who had no husband to experiment on, sat
bolt upright, and looked about her cynically, listening
to the chat that arose as Mrs. Duncombe took her
seat.

"How sweet!" "How true!" "How terrible!"
"How touching!" "What an engaging personal-
ity!" "What a privilege dear Mrs. Van Shuter has
accorded us!" "Those poke-bonnets are rather becoming, don't you think?" "We shall certainly have
to get up something wonderful." "I'm awfully sorry
to leave, but I've got to take little Gladys to the
dentist," and "Are you going on to Mrs. Atterbury's
lunch?"

Rat-tat-tat went the rococo paper-knife. Mrs. Bullion arose to say that in view of the stirring need in
the homes of our laboring sisters Mrs. Duncombe's
able presentation of the facts had manifested, it was
clearly the duty of the ladies here met to organ-
ize themselves into a body to be known by a name
yet to be selected, for the creation and maintenance
of a fund in aid of Mrs. Duncombe's work. Here,

being plucked by the gathers of her gown by Mrs. Van Shuter, who inquired in a loud whisper how long it was going to take, Mrs. Bullion forgot her point, looked vexed, repeated herself in a vague way, and sat down, while Mrs. Boulter, her most intimate enemy, cut in, and proposed to vote Mrs. Van Shuter into the chair which Mrs. Bullion had made sure herself to occupy.

Mrs. Boulter, a beginner in society, who had compiled a birthday book and written pretty Christmas carols, having been next offered and accepted as secretary, Mrs. Bullion, the wife of a famous banker, was in everybody's mind as a fitting treasurer; but on the principle, perhaps, that kings have desired to excel as locksmiths or players upon the flute, Mrs. Bullion had set her affections upon the other post, and was highly miffed at losing it. She made one or two public observations to Mrs. Boulter of an acrimonious type, to which Mrs. Boulter replied airily, and then Mrs. Bullion, with a red face, gathered her street garment about her, and, pleading an immediate engagement, left the room and the committee.

This interruption necessitating whispered consultation of those in chief authority, the general committee took occasion to start an animated discussion as to the best means of raising the money said to be required.

"If I were n't so awfully afraid of the sound of my own voice," said a matron with a family of brunette girls, "I should like to suggest a powder ball at the Madison Square Assembly Rooms, with men and women in purest white, and the tickets ten dollars each. I saw one in London last year, and the effect was positively dream-like."

"A white ball is all very well for women with dark eyes and eyebrows," retorted her interlocutor, a sandy blonde, "but most people look like frights, and you never get the powder out of your hair. Say what you will, nothing pays like amateur theatricals—"

A faint chill fell upon her audience.

"They have never yet paid *me*," said a voice. "I don't know which is worse—to have to sell tickets for them, or to have to go."

"I am sure," retorted the sandy lady, "those in New York have developed the most charming talent. Now, I don't like to mention it, but my daughter has written a three-act play, and *would* do the leading part. Though, of course, we don't *wish* to have her appear in public, she is considered by many to recite 'Les Deux Pigeons' exactly like Bernhardt, and—for such a charity—"

"There is a most deserving person I know who supports her husband and five children by whistling beautifully"—began a benevolent old lady, who could get no hearing, and dropped out.

"How would a Greek play in the original take in New York?" ventured a lady from Boston.

"I'd rather sell for a nigger minstrel show or an amateur circus," answered an experienced vender of tickets, whose authority was law.

"Have we an infant pianist among us?"

"No phenomena, please."

"A bazar?"

"Never."

"A Russian tea?"

"The same old fair disguised."

"Carmencita in a studio?"

"Bernhardt in 'Jean-Marie,' in one of the big draw-ing-rooms?"

"Sarah would know better than to go on the Punch-and-Judy stage at any price—"

Rat-tat-tat went the paper-knife. Mrs. Boulter, speaking for Mrs. Van Shuter, whose bronchitis would not allow her to use her voice, gracefully suggested as treasurer a lady whose support would be of the utmost value to the board, and proposed Mrs. Vernon. That surprised outsider found herself elected before she could say—if she had been inclined to say any-thing so coarse—Jack Robinson.

The color came into Mrs. Vernon's face. She lost her studied suavity of manner, but her protest was overcome. She was placed in a chair near Mrs. Van Shuter, whose fondest wish was now to hurry this thing through. And then the general committee, from whom Mrs. Van Shuter's countenance made no attempt to conceal the fact that she was torpid with fatigue and with hunger for her midday chop, was dismissed, to meet again that day week, at the same hour and—

"Place, shall I say, dear Mrs. Van Shuter?" said the Idol's mouthpiece, in an undertone.

"Oh, I think not," said the chairwoman, disappoint-ingly. "Mrs. Van Loon would have taken them, if she'd been here. Mrs. Bullion would have been the

6*

one, but she 's gone home. I 'm sure I don't know
whom to ask, and I don't think the doctor would like
me to have to think of anything."

"*My* rooms are so ridiculously small," said Mrs.
Boulter, looking at Mrs. Vernon.

Here was Mrs. Vernon's opportunity. Why did she
not avail herself of it? Betty Halliday, observing this,
was fairly puzzled at her reticence.

"Yes, certainly; Mrs. Vernon is the one," said Mrs.
Van Shuter, grasping at relief. "You 'd better tell
them now; it will save Miss Thompson writing little
notes."

"I shall be most happy," said Mrs. Vernon, stiffly,
and, Mrs. Boulter proclaiming the fact, the meeting
broke up in a sea of small talk.

While people were moving (in Mrs. Van Shuter's
eyes far too slowly) to the door, Mrs. Vernon, whose
feelings may have been said to have passed the point
of words, felt her hand taken in the slim brown kid
fingers of Mrs. Calliope Duncombe.

"So you won't speak to me, Luella?" said that
saintly personage. "I did n't think you would go
back on so very old a friend. It gave *me* such pleasure to be of use to *you* to-day."

"It would n't take two words from you, Jane Ketcham," flashed forth a low answer, "to make me come
out before all these women, and tell 'em what you
are."

"No; that you would never do, Luella. How could
you explain — about Judd's Hotel, you know."

"At least, I 'm an honest woman — Oh! I wonder
you have the face — "

"Come, Luella, be nice. Did I, or did n't I, do you a good turn when I suggested having you made the treasurer of this fashionable fund?"

"I don't believe it; if you did, it was to spite me in the end. But there, it is n't the first time—what 'll you take to drop this and clear out?"

"It is n't money I need, but a backing, dear," said the apostle of married women's rights. "And, for the sake of old times, you are going to keep dark about me, are n't you?"

"And you expect me to help you in your frauds— I 'll declare that takes the lead," said the widow, a dangerous look coming into her eyes.

"Sh-sh!" whispered Mrs. Duncombe. "Let us finish this talk another time. Let me come to your fine house to-morrow, and give me lunch, and we 'll find some way to settle the matter to suit you, never fear."

"May I go home with you, Mrs. Vernon?" said Betty Halliday, coming up and ignoring the meek bow of the philanthropist. "I 've a letter from Nell, and other things about which I want to talk."

"Do come," answered the widow, gratefully, while Mrs. Duncombe glided away into the center of a group of women, eager to lavish praises upon her and to receive counsel at her lips.

"That woman!" mused Betty, as they drove off in the brougham. "Where have I seen her face? I 've a vague idea connecting her with the keeper of a bureau for placing teachers, which broke up under a cloud a year or two ago. But I 'm not sure, and I *am* sure Duncombe was not the name. Well, I suppose Mrs. Van Shuter knows where she got her; but to speak frankly, I would n't trust her with the spoons. What I wanted to ask you is if you think Nell and Jerry have suddenly gone mad. My last letter was from the hotel, and here, in this morning's papers, is a 'special despatch' from Florida, stating that Mr. and Mrs. Gerald Vernon are enjoying the hospitalities of Major and Mrs. Shafto at the Bungalow near Bada-joz—"

"It can't be," said the widow, overpowered. She felt to-day as if she were stepping into space.

"That's not all," said Betty. "Among other guests are Miss Kitty Foote, Mr. Carteret Leeds, Mr. Timothy Van Loon, and the celebrated Mrs. Hildegarde de Lancey. There's a choice houseful! I thought, as I dare not tell my mother, you would n't mind telegraphing to Jerry to come home and all will be forgiven. What a 'school for wives' he has taken his to!"

On the day following, a visitor whom Mrs. Vernon's servants had directions to admit touched the button of the electric bell under the stately portal of the corner house where Mrs. Van Shuter had consented to make a call — and where black care had found an entrance, notwithstanding.

Mrs. Calliope Duncombe, delivering up her umbrella and removing her modest overshoes in the presence of Mrs. Vernon's flunkeys, in a wide hall where antique tapestries made a gloom at midday, amid rare carvings and costly ceramics, had a humorous sense of the extremes possible to American fortune within the compass of a quarter of a century. In her mind's

eye, she saw a raw frontier town, of which the chief
center was the tavern kept by Major Judd, known
familiarly as "Buck." She saw the lean "Major"
presiding over the bar, or ushering his patrons into
the long, bare room where two untidy tables were
kept forever covered with spotted cloths, and set with
casters, pitchers, thick goblets, and dingy knives and
forks, with the red or green glasses full of tooth-
picks which formed their ornaments. She saw, issuing from the pantry door and whisking smartly about
these tables, to do the service of the boarders amid
an incense of kitchen smoke, two girls—one spare
and sickly, the other blooming above her sordid surroundings in the effulgence of health and beauty and
animal spirits. She saw the pale girl look with envy
after the rosy one, who shot like a meteor among the
guests, bandying jests, repelling impudence, carrying
all before her.

"If you will please step up into the morning-room,
madam, Mrs. Vernon will see you there," said a portly,
low-voiced functionary, who wore clothes such as old
"Buck" Judd had been married and buried in—but
with a difference.

The mistress of the house was sitting before a wood
fire in the depths of a low arm-chair, the morning's
papers and a handful of notes and cards torn from
their envelopes on the table at her side. Morning
sunlight came warmly through embroidered stuffs of
golden hue, falling over divans and couches, cabinets
and tables, each of its kind the best, and chosen by an
artist to be grouped in this favored interior. The
walls and many shelves and brackets were encumbered

with Mrs. Vernon's well-known collection of "boudoir porcelain," sold in Paris the year before with the effects of a lyric queen, to whom they had been given by their inheritor, a Russian prince. Mrs. Duncombe did not know the value in dollars of this eggshell loveliness glittering softly on every side of her, but it brought to mind a droll suggestion of the stone-china cups and plates and saucers and "sauce-plates" and bird-bath dishes she and Luella used to mop, and drain, and wipe, and put away, till they hated the very sight of them.

Mrs. Vernon wore nothing that was not sent out to her from her man milliner in Paris, who had convinced her that in order fairly to illustrate his genius she must commit no infidelities to his celebrated atelier. Her morning-robe was of an oriental red stuff shaded like the plumage of a bird, bordered with black fur, and over it a sort of surtout of Carmelite black serge, girdled with ropes of gold—a freak of luxury attempting but not quite resigned to go into eclipse. The effect upon her mature beauty was to soften and yet enhance it, and fully justified the whim of the gown's creator. This, again, Calliope Jane's keen gaze made note of, in contrast with the Sunday best of Miss Martha Luella Judd.

Mrs. Vernon had not slept well, and had broken her fast since the night before with only a cup of coffee and a few black Hamburg grapes at nine A. M.; so that she felt absolutely unable to enter, until after luncheon, into a conversation that threatened to be trying at the best. Embarrassed by Mrs. Duncombe's satirical study of herself and surroundings, she took a stitch or two in a table-scarf she was embroidering, dropped it on the floor, drew toward her a Venetian jug of white hyacinths and rearranged the flowers, and finally got up and walked to the window, where she remained, turning her back upon her guest.

"That's it. Keep movin'. Seems more like you, Luella, to be stirrin' around a bit," said Calliope Jane, in an admiring voice.

"Luncheon is served, if you please, madam," said the butler, making a *cavalier-seul* movement within the doorway.

The two ladies sat down in the vast refectory at a table of black oak, square and massive, displaying upon a centerpiece of fair linen edged with convent lace a pierced silver dish containing growing ferns, together with sundry odd devices in silver to hold fruit and sweets, and flagons for claret set in silver openwork.

"My!" said Mrs. Duncombe, in the artless accent of her youth. "You keep a considerable sight o' plated ware, don't you, Luella? And these thin glasses round my plate—I be 'most afraid to touch 'em, for fear they'll fly right out o' my hand."

"Consommé?" said the butler, in her ear.

"What's this in the little cups—tea? No, sir, I'm 'bliged to you; I make it a rule never to fill my stummick up with liquids when I start in to eat. That's a real pritty tidy you've got in the middle of the table, Luella, an' sensible, for I s'pose you ca'late to save your table-cloth clean for dinner, and washin''s powerful dear in New York City."

There were three men in attendance, and a ghost of

a grin hovered over the face of the youngest, at that moment laboriously engaged in carrying a fork from a side-table to a tray. Mrs. Vernon saw it, and her soul waxed hot. She began to talk rapidly, continuously—her visitor, the while, gazing upon her with that enjoying exasperating smile.

"La me suz, Luella," she chimed in, at the first convenient pause. "T' hear your talk *does* carry me back to Judd's. How well I remember your pa sayin' once, 'That gal o' mine, gentlemen, can talk the socks off 'n anybody I ever see.'"

Mrs. Vernon started, dropped her napkin, and reclaimed it with a shaking hand. It was not the matter only, but the manner of the speech. Not the least of Mrs. Duncombe's accomplishments was her inimitable faculty of reproducing tones.

"Often and often," pursued the visitor, pensively, "I think I can see the old man sittin' in his shirt-sleeves, under the drinkin'-water bucket, with his feet on the railin' of the hotel-poach, and gittin' up every now and then to go back into the bar. Don't you remember, when he 'd had about enough, an' was feelin' real good, how he 'd always shut one eye an' say: 'I 'm a plain Blue Grass man, boys; ain't got no book-larnin', an' git my relijun onst a year reg'lar—but I was bawn an' raised in the finest country on God's yeth, an' don't you forget it, nuther'?"

Mrs. Vernon was spared witnessing the effect of this impersonation, by the disappearance behind the screen of two of her servants, while the butler kept discreetly at her back. She emptied· her water-glass, and bestowed a pleading look upon her relentless guest.

"The stage loses an accomplished actress in you, Jane," she said. "I wonder you don't try giving character sketches in people's drawing-rooms. It would surely be a success, and—perhaps—a *safer* method of securing what you want."

"What! you advise it!" said Calliope, beaming. "I am certain you 'd recognize my models, if no one else found me out. But don't trouble your head about me, dear. I 'm doing splendidly, thanks to the kind ladies of New York society, who are always in want of an outlet for their zeal."

The dreadful meal proceeded to its close, and Mrs. Duncombe having afforded, as it were, a sample of her skill, relaxed her efforts in that particular line of torment. When the two women were again alone, Mrs. Vernon, with a sudden departure from her attempted indifference, confronted her opponent boldly.

"Was your life in the House of Correction, while you were serving a two-years' sentence for getting money under false pretences, so much to your taste that you want to go back to it, Jane?"

"I am the widow of a Union soldier who died for his country at Antietam," said Calliope, dropping her eyes. "And if I seek to eke out my modest pension of eight dollars a month from the Government by the use of the talents with which God has gifted me—"

"Rubbish!" interrupted the other. "Come, now, there 's no use wasting my time. I know you, root and branch, Jane Ketcham; and when I saw you, yesterday, sitting up among all those women you had taken in, looking like the cat that had been at the cream, I made my mind up, *straight*."

"To do what, Luella?" asked Calliope, still meekly.

"To force you to back out of this business without open scandal, as you suspected when you saw me, or you would n't have tried getting me upon the board to be a party to your fraud."

"Now you are getting angry, dear, and in your tantrums you always lose your grip. Just keep calm, and consider what exposing me will do for you. It 'll be a thousand times worse for the public to have a full account *now* of your life as a table-girl at Judd's, where old Vernon picked you up and married you, than it would have been before your son made his aristocratic match. Now, just as you are getting into the Four Hundred, fancy it! And I think you may trust me, love, to do the thing thoroughly when I set out to have my revenge."

"And I have given—not paid—you hundreds of dollars—would have done anything—to keep you a decent woman," cried the widow, whose passion, long repressed, had by this time burst its bounds. She broke into a storm of weeping, at which Calliope looked serenely on. When Luella "lost her grip," it had always been the advance signal of Calliope's success. In this paroxysm, the untamed creature hinted at in the smiling portrait below-stairs revealed herself without restraint.

"There—there, Luella," said the visitor, at last. "You 'll cry yourself down sick, you know you will. Take the thing quietly, as I do. Lord knows, you 've got lots to comfort you."

"Will no money pay you to give this up, and leave New York?"

"WHEN LUELLA 'LOST HER GRIP.'"

"Judging from appearances, I shall soon command what will supply my necessities for the present. But can't you understand—you, Luella, who have made such a struggle to know the right sort? It is social place, the regard of the community, I need most, now. Six months ago, I was, under the lowly name of Madame Isaacson, an astrologist in Boston, telling fortunes at twenty-five cents each; and, my dear, I nearly starved. Now—well, you saw for yourself how the great ladies of Gotham swarmed around me. Do you suppose I mean to renounce all this until—when—I am obliged?"

"You are a shameless wretch," said the widow, between her teeth. "I should like to call a policeman and have you put out of my house."

"But you won't, love. I know you. You have n't moral courage enough for that. Ah, it was always such a relief, Luella, to talk freely before you."

"What do you mean to do?"

"What do *you* mean to do? If you can't be satisfied to keep quiet, and patronize me with the rest of your swell friends, I should almost suggest *your* leaving town, instead of me."

Poor Mrs. Vernon, to whom this episode was but the culmination of many trials from the same source, looked at her old acquaintance in dismay. Leave town! Now, at the moment of Gerald's return with the young wife who was to be her most powerful lever in forcing her way upward! When her entertainments for the bridal pair, that were intended to conquer all lingering opposition to her advance, were planned and waiting! Now, when her lip was on

7

the cup! The climax of her tragic comedy was reached.

"Me leave town?" she said, suddenly dropping into the dialect of a distant but not forgotten past. "Well, of all the impudence! I'll tell you what, Jane Ketcham, I have had my fill of this. Walk out of my house this minute, and never set foot in it again."

"I am going, dear," murmured the invincible Jane; "though, seeing you have n't been troubled with me in two years, you might have had a little more patience now. But before I go, Luella, let me warn you that the best way out of your present complications is to —let me see—have a sudden indisposition before the next meeting of the board, and resign because your physician has advised a change of air."

"This, then, is your little game? This is what you wanted from the first?"

"If we can't work together, we are best apart, certainly," said Jane, drawing her veil over her poke-bonnet, and buttoning the brown gloves. "Might I ask that butler of yours where he put my silk umbrella —a testimonial of esteem from an Ibsen class I had at a summer resort a little while ago? I think your butler has a soul for the drama, Luella, for his face was eloquent with appreciation while I impersonated your poor dear papa. Good-by, again, and don't trouble to see me to the door. I shall not be surprised to hear of your leaving town before I 've a chance to visit you again."

VII

"ON time," said Gerald, consulting his watch, as the Washington express slackened speed in the station at Jersey City. " Come, Nell—has that woman got your bag and wraps? Hughes will go on ahead to find the carriage on the other side—I 'll swear it 's a jolly thing to fill one's lungs again with our own North River air."

Eleanor, quietly, and with a lagging step, kept at her husband's side as they followed the throng on the platform, through the ferry-house to the boat, thence to the forward deck, where she leaned against the rail and gazed over at the roofs and spires of her birth-place, quitted some short two months before. Jerry, growing more exhilarated as the salt breeze swept from him the remnants of stale railway smoke, hardly glanced at her. His thoughts had sprung forward with a bound to his old familiar life and association with other men, interrupted by an episode that, however charming, was now parcel of the past. A hundred images of his active, popular, buoyant young manhood swarmed around him, and tickled his imagination with the joy of return into their broad arena.

99

When he caught sight, standing against the opposite railing, and eying him without appearing to wish to do so, of a man whom he had known at a club to which both belonged, having but a tepid liking for him hitherto, his heart expanded into radiant friendship for the more recent dweller in the scenes to which he was going back.

"Why, that's Telfair," he said to Eleanor, with animation. "He's been to Washington about the Stryker case, of course. If you don't mind my leaving you a minute,—you are all right here,—I'll be back at once. I'd like to find out from Telfair how that Stryker business is likely to come out."

Eleanor smiled, nodding assent. When he left her, she turned her back on the crowd and leaned over the rail, staring down into the green combs of the waves, trying to keep hot tears out of her eyes. During the latter part of their journey, the unconscious Gerald had shown her plainly the sort of relief he felt in getting back. As if to make up for it, he had redoubled endearments, and was again the bright, fascinating fellow who had wooed her, the fond young husband of the earliest married days. He had done his best to atone for the frequent shows of petulance, of boyish tyranny, that had come thick and fast since the unfortunate day of their arrival at the Bungalow.

That visit! Eleanor's cheeks crimsoned again at thought of it. She would have liked to blot out forever the memory of her hysterical pleading with her husband to take her away on the morrow after the scene of the midnight ballet; of his vexed, then angry, remonstrance against her prudishness; of her dismay when she found that, in the fast society the home-bred, pure-minded girl found so offensive to her instincts, he was not only at home but admirably entertained.

Eleanor vanquished, but not convinced, they had stayed on at the Bungalow until after the first limit fixed. The four days of it had been forty in her sight. A letter from Gerald's mother, urging him to return home, had added to his impatience of feminine restraint. He accused Eleanor of being in league with his mother to keep him in leading-strings, and put the offending missive in the fire. And Mrs. Shafto had somehow become aware of all these petty infelicities, and had ventured to counsel and sympathize with Nell, while giving Gerald opportunities to calm his excitement in the soothing society of his fair friend Hildegarde.

Hildegarde! Eleanor hated herself for dwelling ever so lightly on an uncomfortable feeling that had sprung up in her mind at Badajoz. She had put it aside, and trampled on the base temptation to misjudge her husband. Did not Gerald come back to her from Hildegarde's companionship, swearing that poor dear creature was very pitiful, ringing the changes on her wrongs, but that he had learned to prefer a woman with a future to a woman with a past, and was content to leave the task of consolation to Mr. Timothy Van Loon? Was not Hildegarde herself all that was tender, sympathetic, admiring, to Eleanor? For Mrs. Shafto Nell had conceived a dislike that did not lessen upon acquaintance. But Mrs. de Lancey, in her refined gentleness, her winning deprecation of unkind judgment—what was she but a flower beaten from

7*

its stalk by a tempest? One must be warped by un-
worthy prejudice indeed to have such fancies as occasionally crept into Eleanor's brain concerning her.
Ah, well—whatever Jerry's offenses were, they had
always been met in loving condonation by his wife.
To her, every hair of his head was now dear with a
tenderness unimagined in her girlhood. They were
on their way to the new home, where the world was
to be shut out, and they two were to reign supreme.
Everything that fortune could do to lend external
brightness to their lives had been done; why, then,
did Eleanor sigh again at the close of her reverie?
Jerry returned to her as the boat drew in to the slip.

"Telfair 's a capital fellow," he said in great good
humor. "He 's been telling me all that 's gone on
about town and at the clubs. Seems to me we 've
been away a thousand years. There 's Hughes gone
ahead, and your new footman waiting near the gang-
plank, Mrs. Vernon. Blest if I remember the fellow's
name, do you? Nell, I 'm afraid we 'll be a regular
pair of Veneerings—that couple in Dickens, don't
you know?—in our new house, with the new servants and horses, and all that. I wonder which of
the family will be there. I don't believe my mother 'll
come, but I hardly think yours will be able to keep
away—why, what a long face you have! Not a bit
what it ought to be."

Nell forced a smile in answer to his rattling chal-
lenge. She was thinking: "Oh, I hope mama won't
see me till I 've had a chance to get over this little
doleful fit, for which there is no reason. She 'd be
so quick to read my face; and Betty's eyes are so

sharp, and dear Trix loves me so, I could n't bear for them to imagine I 'm not the happiest woman in the world."

Even when leaning back on the cushioned lining of her brougham,—that "dark myrtle-green satin" Trix and she had so often pictured as the limit of their luxurious desires,—Eleanor's mind had not regained its normal calm. She felt ashamed of herself that the home-coming, so happy in anticipation, should be thus clouded; and with a strong effort lent herself to Jerry's joyous mood.

To him, the squalor of the down-town region through which his high-stepping cobs minced daintily, as if despising it, was full of renewed interest.

With the zest of the returning cockney, he inhaled the faded air of the dull thoroughfares pregnant with the smell of over-ripe foreign fruits, clothing of hurrying crowds, contents of shops open to the sidewalk, black slime of uncleaned streets. He looked up at the skeleton trestlework along which the elevated trains went incessantly whizzing overhead, with satisfaction, as a symbol of the busy metropolitan life. The roar overhead, the rumble of trucks upon the granite, the ceaseless swarming of eager pedestrians, the tinkle of street-car bells, the cries of children playing on the sidewalk amid all this hurly-burly, the shouts over repeated blockings of the way by a mass of vehicles, —all blending to swell the chant of a great city in business hours,— to Jerry were welcome music.

"What a change from our sylvan solitudes!" Eleanor said, with another sigh.

"Change! I should think so," he answered cheerily. "Why, you silly girl, you did n't expect to go on philandering for a year and a day, did you? We 're part of the community now; come back to take our place in actual life, out of our lovers' paradise, that had to end."

That had to end! Poor foolish Nell, her young heart straining to hold on to its ideals, felt her eyes fill with tears. There are times when listening to common sense is like lying down upon paving-stones.

Soon they had left the haunts of work-a-day, and come out into Fifth Avenue at an hour when the leisure world was in full enjoyment of a brilliant afternoon in spring. From victorias and open landaus rolling toward them head after head inclined in gracious salutation. Men, determinately appareled after Piccadilly modes, wearing well-made cheviot bodycoats, well-kempt silk hats, well-chosen flowers in their buttonholes, carrying sticks, and walking in the long, easy stride of the patrician idlers of Park Row, bowed to them from the sidewalks, whence also came airy greetings from a larger number of the other sex who have no need to seek Mayfair models to turn themselves out in the prettiest dress-parade in Christendom.

On such an afternoon the thoroughfare of New York's fashion is at its best. The huge buildings of cream-colored and of buff brick, with their delicate traceries and finials of carvings, which have been erected by modern art to take away our reproach of monotonous brownstone, seem to catch and throw off the sunlight. Many houses in the older and lower part have their strips of green turf dight with pansies and English daisies. Flowers are everywhere: in the bonnets, in posies worn upon the breast, behind windows where Easter lilies rear their pure crests, in balconies and boxes, in street-barrows, in the baskets of humbler venders. Roses, azaleas, hyacinths, geraniums, ferns, appear to be loitering on call. From Washington Square to Madison Square, where leaves have just ventured from winter bondage, and in the green precincts of which the busy New York day stands still to breathe awhile, as on both sides of the long avenue to the Plaza, nearly two miles and a half in all, there is a never-ending procession of pedestrians, who in temper illustrate frankly the American virtues of good humor and self-respect, as they push ahead, amused at the passing show of the vehicles of luxury and pleasure that throng between.

In a side-street west of Fifth Avenue Mr. and Mrs. Gerald Vernon's home revealed itself by a blush of newly painted brick, a series of crisp muslin curtains veiling the four rows of windows, a variety of new brass- and iron-work and plate-glass about the swinging doors of the vestibule, and balcony-boxes newly filled with daisies and myosotis.

When they stopped by the curbstone, Gerald, conscious of a shamefaced desire to avoid the notice of possible observers in Numbers 14 and 18, glanced about him nervously before inviting his bride to alight. But in the cold-blooded current of town life, where the casualties of birth, death, and marriage pass often unheard of by an adjoining neighbor, their home-coming was unnoticed save by an Italian gentleman grinding with maddening deliberation from a barrel-organ, "Down went McGinty to the bottom of the sea, Dressed in his best suit of clothes," whose smile, as he doffed his hat, was conventionally blank.

"But for the precedent," said Gerald, "I'd give that fellow twenty-five cents for treating us like regular old married hacks. No! basta, signor, allez-vous-en —get out, for Heaven's sake! Now, Nell, if you don't say this is better than a Florida hotel!"

With a word of shy greeting to her new domestic staff, Eleanor went from room to room, suspecting Trix in ambush, her heart warm with the thought that mama might be hidden behind some portière. Evidences of their loving work were everywhere: in the ordering of furniture as Nell liked it, in the judicious distribution of bridal gifts. Up-stairs, in a sunny room where Nell's books and Gerald's met upon low shelves, a divan was revealed whereon Jerry's lazy length might sprawl; Nell's wicker chair stood on a bearskin by the tea-table, before a couple of logs burning softly in the fireplace of ivory tiles, and here the married pair brought their explorations to a halt.

"They must have just left the house," Eleanor said, with a burst of girlish tenderness. "Oh! Jerry darling, how much better home people's love is than anything the world can give you if it tries!"

"Hullo! They've got all my old college pictures in here," Jerry rejoined, well pleased. "What's that scratching under the sofa, Nell? By George, I believe it's Nip."

And Nip it was, Trix's second self, her inseparable fox-terrier, who, with a muffled bark, darted out from beneath a couch, sliding partly on his head, in his effort to be rid of a note tied to his collar with a large orange bow.

"It 's from Trix, of course. Be still, Nip dear, till I get it off," cried Eleanor, as Nip bounded into her lap in rapturous welcome and desire to be rid of his encumbrance.

Read the young couple, cheek to cheek:

My dearest Nell and Jerry: What it will cost me to sneak out the basement way as you go up the front steps you can never know, but mama and Betty have left me here till the last minute, making me promise not to show an eyelash when you come. You are to have your first dinner to yourselves; and there are sweetbreads, and birds, and little things that you can't have *every day*, I know, and that Nip and I *just love*. We have been in the kitchen interviewing the cook, and there 's nothing we 've not found out. Mind, don't be at the table a minute after eight, for we are all coming then, and I 've so much to say, I can't hold it in — oh! I 'm just *dying* to stay and talk. Nip knows this is your house, for he has gone under the sofa and is about to take a nap, as I told him, and he would never do that in any stranger's. So welcome, welcome, welcome home, from your ever loving

TRIX.

P. S. — We 've got places for all the wedding presents but Mrs. Cranston's bothering clock, and that 's in the third story back. Cousin Sarah's vase is on the lowest shelf of the Indian cabinet, where nobody can see it. Old Norah would break her heart if you did n't use her crazy-quilt, so I 've put it on your lounge, and I know you 'll let it stay.

N. B. — La cuisinière est peu aimable envers mon cher Nip, et je la déteste; mais n'importe, la *vieille chose* ne peut pas lire ceci!

Where now were Eleanor's fears, tremors, sad remembrances? Vanished, swept away by a heartening

breeze.   When eight o'clock brought with it her dear
ones, the first evening at home closed in unbroken
peace, even though Jerry, who had promised to finish
it with his mother, bade her not trouble to sit up for
him, as he might look in later at the club.

"I hope Mrs. Vernon is not feeling seriously ill,"
said Mrs. Halliday, who had made up her mind to
inaugurate the new era with all that was needful in
the way of Christian suavity.

"I don't know—I imagine not," Jerry answered
shortly.   He had not recovered from the letter of rebuke for taking his wife to Badajoz, and in his heart
thought his mother was sulking at home to punish
him.

VIII

HE second meeting of the "Woman's Society for the Legal Relief of Oppressed Wives," after various delays, took place, not at the house of Mrs. Vernon, whose physician had declared that lady totally unable to bear the strain of further participancy in work for the public good, but at the mansion of no less a dignitary than Mrs. Van Loon, born in the American purple, married in early youth to a great fortune, and backed by an actual pedigree as respectable and solid as any in the land. How this came about may be briefly explained.

Mrs. Van Loon, who, at the time of the first meeting, had been on her way across the continent from Santa Barbara (whither she had taken Mr. Van Loon for the benefit of his ailing throat), arrived in town to hear how clever Mrs. Boulter had succeeded in wresting the reins of power from Mrs. Bullion, and was in a fair way to control the most fashionable charity of the year. This to Mrs. Van Loon was wormwood. More than once she had had occasion to bow her neck and come in to Mrs. Boulter's schemes. Mrs. Boulter, clever as she was, had no birth, and little or no money; and Mrs. Van Loon viewed with displeasure the encroachment of mere brains and glibness upon a territory hitherto almost exclusively her own. When it was a question of laying down the social law, Mrs. Van Loon felt herself to be deputed by Heaven to do it. And if you once let these writing people get ahead in society, in Heaven's name, where will they stop?

A call upon Mrs. Van Shuter found that exhausted leader willing to waive all rights of government in favor of her younger and more active ally. Mrs. Vernon's polite note to inform Mrs. Van Shuter, and the ladies of the board, of her great regret that the orders of her physician made it imperative for her to withdraw from connection with the work, gave Mrs. Van Loon the immediate opportunity she desired. Mrs. Van Shuter, who agreed to attend the meetings if she were released from further effort, made her last contribution to the fund by ordering the hapless Miss Thompson to write an entirely new set of little notes. And clever Mrs. Boulter found herself bidden into an enemy's camp, where judicious wire-pulling put Mrs. Van Loon in the chair, *vice* Mrs. Van Shuter, resigned, and where Mrs. Bullion, now mysteriously appeased, was induced to reconsider and to accept the office of treasurer.

In the hands of Mrs. Van Loon the committee was as wax. The chairwoman let the dark-eyed lady suggest her *bal poudré;* the sandy-haired lady was allowed to air her histrionic daughter; all other schemes, from the Russian tea to the amateur nigger minstrels, were vouchsafed a gracious hearing; and then the obedi-

ent assemblage was somehow made to understand
that it was pledged to support an Early-Republican
ball, to be opened by a Centennial Minuet.

"It is so simple," said the presiding officer. "Every
one should wear ancestral clothes belonging to the
period, with miniatures, and seals, and—er—all that
kind of thing—and the hair powdered, as Mrs.
Creighton so happily suggests. Those who dance in
the opening minuet should, of course, represent families known in political or social life in the days of
Washington's residence in New York as President.
By hunting up all the old books at the Historical and
Society and Astor libraries, many valuable hints may
be obtained as to emblems and mottos and decorations of that date. And I have an idea that our best
people might be induced to form a loan collection of
the portraits of their American ancestors to hang
around the walls of the ball-room, if the insurance
were properly looked after, and there were detectives
kept day and night, of course. What could be easier?"

Easy as it was, an unaccountable dejection settled
over certain portions of the company. At once a buzz
of discussion ensued; and the wheels of progress
stopped. The burning question that arose in every
woman's mind as to the award of places in the minuet
of honor banished all thought of the "Legal Relief
of Oppressed Wives"; the object of the meeting was
forgotten. Mrs. Boulter, after letting fly two or three
arrows of satire that pierced Mrs. Van Loon's armor
visibly, offered her resignation to the board. Mrs.
Gramercy St. John, who was deemed sure of a leading rôle in the affair, confided to her neighbor that

she could not bring herself to serve, because Mrs.
Fulton Manhattan (whose great-grandfather had sold
figs while hers stood on the balcony beside President
Washington at Federal Hall) had been proposed as
her vis-à-vis. Mrs. Fulton Manhattan, hearing this
whisper, also resigned from the board of managers.
Old Mrs. Bowling Green, whose spinster daughter
Selina had been overlooked in the first hastily made
list of dancers, rose up, and in a quavering voice
begged leave to offer a few remarks. She would de-
tain the ladies only long enough to say that although
her ancestor was a favorite staff-officer of Washington, and the cups from which his Excellency drank
tea with her grandmama were daily dusted upon her
cupboard-shelves, she should consider it quite too
ridiculous to have one of her family appear in such
a *mixed* affair—after which she left the room. Mrs.
Central Parker, who had been absorbed in the mental
wording of a cablegram to Worth for a delicious
First-Empire toilet, sprang upon her feet at this, and,
resenting a fancied direction of Mrs. Green's remarks
to her, proffered *her* resignation, and retired, resolv-
ing to induce her husband to cable, instead, for a
duke's house for the London season.

Amid this confusion, and under a stress of feeling
that bid fair to depopulate the committee, Mrs. Calliope Duncombe sat by, serene and unruffled, her eyes
cast down, her meek hands folded in her lap. Something in her expression seemed to annoy Mrs. Van
Shuter, who was in the condition of the camel that
resented the last straw.

"I think it would be as well to tell that person,—

Mrs. What 's-er-name,— " said the Idol, very crossly and audibly, to Mrs. Van Loon, "that it 's of no earthly use for *her* to come to the meetings of our committee."

"Certainly," said Mrs. Van Loon; "I had thought of that, myself. It 's bad enough to be in such a turmoil, without having anybody sitting by and looking like a saint. Tell her when we 've anything to give, we 'll let her know."

"But I never tell people things, myself," answered the great lady, a-flutter; "it is so apt to bring on palpitation, to have to think about the words."

"Then the secretary must notify her. What with the clatter and quarreling, I 'm almost distracted now," said the chairwoman of the board.

BETTY HALLIDAY, again in attendance upon an occasion she vowed was as good as a circus with three rings, gave a full report of the proceedings to Nell at luncheon, where Nell's mother-in-law had dropped in on her way for her drive. Betty, struck with the careworn look on Mrs. Vernon's face, thought she observed her eye gleam with something like triumph at the account of the snub to Mrs. Duncombe. But the widow, observing merely that it was really too bad she should have to miss the Early-Republican ball, as she had more than half decided to go to the other side, bestowed a kiss upon Nell's cheek, and took an imposing leave.

ELEANOR, who objected to the idea of set afternoons at home, on which her pretty house would be

8

overrun by the crowd that comes to congratulate and goes to criticize, had at once established a tea-table at five o'clock, where friends dropping in were tempted to linger with the lengthening days.

She was not a woman like the heroines of French novels, to make intimate corners into which it is death for more than one man to venture at a time. There was in her drawing-room an absence of divans, beneath tent-shaped draperies pitched under palm-trees where camels and caravans alone are wanting. Visitors, presenting themselves in visiting-hours, had no opportunity to discern their hostess in the rose-ate glow of lamps veiled by wonderful frilled shades, lolling on piles of cushions in a Delsartian pose, tête-à-tête with some youngster who assumes to be disagreeably surprised at an interruption. Her own old friends,—men and girls,—and Jerry's coterie of gilded youths, who had been a little everywhere, knew a little of everything, dealt with all topics lightly, often amusingly, pronounced Nell's "five o'clock" a find.

"'What makes the lambs love Mary so?'" said Dick Henderson, on one of these afternoons. "Do you give it up, Mrs. Jerry? Well, its hostess apart, yours is a restful house. The amount of manual labor a man has, nowadays, in calling upon most women! The logs that won't burn, the chimneys that smoke, the candle-shades that catch fire, the spirit-lamps and dogs that have to be put out—"

"Don't, please," said Trix, coming in, in her walk-ing-dress, just then. "You make me ashamed of my dear Friar Tuck, who, when he goes with me visiting,

will neither stay outside nor stay in. Nell, if I'm
later than usual, put it down to Tuck, for he had to
be exercised. Ever since the awful day he—well, not
exactly growled, but—*rumbled* at Jerry's Aunt Tryphena, who despises dogs, I've never dared bring him
here, without coming in first to reconnoiter. He's
walking around the block, waiting for me, now, the
dear."

"What, alone?" said Eleanor.

"No; there's somebody else," the girl answered,
blushing and vanishing amid a general laugh, to re-
appear, accompanied not only by a noble St. Bernard
dog, who at once laid his "Shaksperean dewlaps" on
Mrs. Gerald's knees, and stood still to be caressed,
but a slim, broad-shouldered young man wearing an
altogether bright and wholesome countenance, who
was introduced to her sister as Mr. Vyvan.

IX

HIS little group brought with it into Eleanor's drawing-room a sense of open-air freshness and young vitality. The blitheness in Vyvan's face set Eleanor to thinking; and, placing him in a chair beside her, she studied him narrowly, a scrutiny his frank manhood enabled the youth to bear becomingly. Trix, meanwhile, came in for her share of rallying attention.

"It 's love me, love my dog, with you, is n't it, Miss Beatrix?" said De Witt, in a low tone, as he handed her the cream.

"Not always," the girl answered, curling her lip; "*you* are at perfect liberty to love my dog, Mr. de Witt."

"Hard hit, Freddy," said Henderson. "Come here, Friar Tuck, you are a credit to your bringing up. Short 's your friend, not Codlin. Would it insult you to be offered one of Mrs. Jerry's tea-cakes?"

But the Friar, proof against blandishments, had now transferred his huge muzzle from Nell's knee to Vyvan's, where he remained, consulting the young man's face with the dumb lovingness a big dog can make so eloquent.

"Did n't he take a prize at the last bench-show?"
went on Henderson with persistent civility to Trix.

"No-o," said Tuck's mistress, shaking her head as
she surveyed her treasure mournfully. "I can't think
why, but I 'm afraid there was something underhand,
because one of the judges told me Tuck was too perfectly lovely to live."

"I admire that fellow's diplomacy," put in De Witt.
"Did he tell you also that you should have a dog-
show exclusively for Friar Tuck, where all the others
would be cats, and he 'd be sure to win a prize—"

Trix was saved the trouble of a repartee by Friar
Tuck himself, who, turning at this moment his deliberate gaze on the last speaker, vented his feelings by
a long and heartfelt yawn.

"You have been very lucky to win the Friar's confidence," Eleanor said to young Vyvan. "He is, in
general, very repellant of advances by strangers."

"Oh, I was brought up with dogs for playfellows.
In the South, where our doors are always open, they
walk through our homes like members of the family.
I pity these poor creatures cribbed up in town.
I suppose it 's the fellow-feeling that makes me
kind."

"Then you miss your Southern life? But of course
you do. My sister Trix and I, and our brother Jack,
have been going always in summer to a rather hot,
dull little place my mother has on the Hudson River,
and we preferred that to anything New York could
furnish. Those splendid big Maryland estates of
yours must give you even more of a feeling of room
to breathe and grow in."

8*

"Big enough they are," said Brock, laughing; "but the splendor is all in space and forests."

"Tell me about your home."

"I sha'n't bore you? It's an old place called Mount St. Dunstan, that has been built on a long time, and has always belonged to my mother's family. After my father was killed in the last year of the war, I was born, and she went back there to live with my grandfather, who is now a very old man, devoted to flowers and dogs. Every fine day you may see him working in his garden or greenhouses, with a golden collie at his heels. My mother keeps the house, with a poor lot of servants,—the best they can get down there now,—and everything indoors is rather worn and shabby, I suppose; but I know I would n't have it changed—"

His ingenuous face, one of those in which expression is "on tiptoe for a flight," softened, then clouded as he stopped.

"You are the only son?" Eleanor asked softly.

"The only child, worse luck. It is hard for her to do without me, though of course there are always cousins stopping in the house, and work enough in the affairs of the plantation. And she is getting used to it, now, what with the four years at the university and those in New York."

"We must try to make you feel at home with us," she said, with a smile that reminded him of Trix.

"Oh, I am happy. I like the vista that seems to have no end that opens before a young man of purpose here. When I first came, I had such a different notion of standards and values—coming out of that dreamy old-world atmosphere of sentimental aris-

tocracy into this broad daylight of commercial enterprise. Now I have found my place, I am encouraged
about the future in a way I could not have been, had
I remained at home. But, Mrs. Vernon, you must
think me abominably vain."

"Some day I must hear more. You must come
and dine with us," she began, when her attention was
claimed elsewhere.

"Come, Mrs. Jerry, decide for us," said Henderson.
"Is it the men's fault or the girls', that we average
fellows in society have to wait till our hair gets thin
before we take wives?"

"Like old Beau Meredith," added De Witt; "live
to be the happiness of successive generations of débu-
tantes, and return to second childhood in the process.
But it's poor economy to wait till your hair grows
thin before you marry. One of the prettiest women
I know told me she never sees the bald spot on her
husband's head that it does n't make her want to
gape. Of course it's the women's fault. They won't
look at us unless we can give them — well, say, — "
looking about him approvingly, — "the likes of this."

"That's it," said Henderson, ruefully. "Fancy asking any girl of our set to live with you and be your
love in a flat with five speaking-trumpets surmount-
ing five visiting-cards in the vestibule, and a smell of
codfish in the halls. I've often thought I might
manage to *feed* my wife, if she would make her trousseau last; but how I could pay three dollars an evening for cabs to convey her to other people's dinners,
I don't see. On the whole, I think I had rather be
taken in and done for by my father-in-law."

"Widows, now," said De Witt, "offer a delightful

solution of the difficulty, if they are rich and young; but the stock is limited."

"For shame!" said Eleanor. "I refuse to arbitrate. Thank goodness, there are love-matches, even in 'our set.'"

"Denzil's, for instance," said Henderson. "When he left college, an honor-man, and the world before him where to choose,—the best-looking, the cleverest fellow of his day, an athlete, and a hero,—he went in for architecture, and might have been anything. Well, two years later, he took out to dinner a girl with a Burne-Jones profile and without a cent, raved the next day to us about her brow that should have worn a perpetual fillet, and in three months—married her. Look at them now. They have been married eight years. She is a dowdy goddess, a millstone around Denzil's neck. He has lost pluck and temper, has become a cynic, pitches into all things American, is begrudging of other men's good things, and continually hampered by the necessity of paying household bills. Now tell me, whose happiness does Denzil make? Who makes his? What has *he* secured by marrying for love?"

"*That* Mrs. Denzil!" commented Trix, scornfully. "She is the kind of limp woman who sits and complains of her husband, and raves about Browning and Tolstoi, while her children are running in the streets. It is her fault, if anybody's; and I think you are all horrid and cold-blooded in the way you talk."

"Have you ever estimated the price of the butcher's meat consumed by Nip and Tuck, Miss Beatrix?" said her tormentor, Fred de Witt. "And do you think you 'd be willing to put down your dogs, as some women put down their carriages, for your husband's sake ?"

"There is something else I should like to put down first," said Trix, crushingly.

To this chatter Brock Vyvan listened with mingled feelings. He knew these men to belong to a class of comparative leisure, to be well-dressed, able to indulge themselves in many things which he could but dream of one day possessing. He saw them drifting out of youth without a thought of assuming the matrimonial yoke, and he could not but admit a certain reason in their arguments against so doing. Even with the ring of Trix's honest voice in protest in his ear, he looked around him, and then in fancy back to the faded rooms of the Mount St. Dunstan homestead which was to be his inheritance. In contrast with this affluent prosperity deemed indispensable to the higher civilization of to-day, he set the barren acres, the cramped fortunes, the lack of ready money of his home-people. He thought of how many years of toil must pass to bring him to the independence needed to rid the old place of debt, to furnish comforts to his mother's declining years; and steeled his heart against the siren whisperings that had, of late, begun to echo there with a music that never ceased.

Eleanor, refusing to "give in her testimony," felt that on her side much might be said. "It is a craven sort of thing," she thought, "to sit here and let these young men think we are all material worldlings because we 've been born in a certain social class. But I can't speak; the truth is, I 'm afraid to say too

much. And they might not believe me if I told the
very truth—that if Jerry had brought me nothing
but himself I 'd have been as content. And if this is
foolish, I don't want to be wise."

The talk was here interrupted by Hughes, the ex-
valet, who for an increase of stipend had consented
to take upon his accomplished hands the duty of butler in the new establishment. He was preceding two
gentlemen, about whom Trix, recognizing them, uttered her significant word, "Bother!" as Hughes announced Mr. Van Loon and Mr. Leeds.

The blood came into Eleanor's cheeks. The immense impertinence of the individual last named, in
intruding himself under the wing of an old acquaintance into her house, filled her with indignation that
found no vent. It is in comedies of the stage, not of
real life, that the heroine has the exact words ready
with which to repel audacity. And a woman in her
own house rarely allows herself the pleasure of a
downright invitation to go out of it to any one short
of an intending burglar. Even a book-agent's way
to the front door is soothed by apologetic courtesy.

"Saw Vernon at the club," said Timothy, address-
ing his hostess, but his vagrant eye captured anew by
the spring-like charms of Trix, who had given him a
slight and frosty nod. "Said you 'd be here at tea-
time. Got in from Florida on my boat, this morning.
Havin' a new yacht built, and, by Jove, I 'd thought
o' namin' it the *Beatrix;* but your sister 's so uncommon huffy, nowadays—won't look at a man, like the
other girls you see around. Have you heard my
latest good thing anywhere? No? Really! New

beauty at the Ponce de Leon since you left, named Milliken, from the West somewhere, stands six foot in her stockin's, if an inch. Can't think what 's happened to the girls now, to make 'em all so tall. Fellows wanted me to lead a cotillion with the Milliken; but I just looked at her, and gave it up. 'Could n't do it unless I danced on stilts,' I said, 'and I never learned that way.' By Jove, I 've heard of nothin' else since, everywhere I 've been. People are buzzin' it all over the country, I believe. 'Could n't do it unless I danced on stilts' was what I *said*, 'and I never learned that way.' I believe somebody has sent the thing to 'Puck'; but you may say you had it right from me."

Trix laughed. Encouraged by what he took to be approval, Mr. Van Loon forsook Eleanor, and conveyed himself and hat and stick over to a pianobench near where the girl was seated, his place by Mrs. Gerald being at once assumed by Mr. Carteret Leeds.

"Van Loon told you we 'd–er–met Vernon at the club," said that unabashed gentleman. "From what he said, I–er–thought you 'd be glad of the last news from our friends in Florida. Your husband told us he 'd be at home, himself, this afternoon; but I suppose he changed his mind, as I saw him walkin' with–er–a fair lady down the avenue a half-hour since."

"Mr. Vernon is in the habit of going to his mother at this time," said Eleanor, angry with herself for answering at all.

"Oh, no; not Mrs. Vernon," he said, with an intonation maliciously jocose—" not Mrs. Vernon, certainly.   I say, it would be a good joke on Jerry to let the cat out now."

" You have taken many liberties," Eleanor said very low, and with awful distinctness, " but you have never gone so far before as to presume to discuss my husband's affairs with me.   May I ask that you will keep this fact in mind ? "

" Oh, but I say, you know," he urged, still jocular, "most women would be glad of a chance to bring a man to book—when it 's about an old flame, especially.   Come, now, I 'll lay ten to one you 're dyin' to get down off your high horse and own up you 're curious.   But I won't peach.   Only you 'd better ask *Jerry why he advised Van Loon to come to see you now.*"

They were sitting a little apart, behind the table in the back-room, and, with an exclamation of disgust, Eleanor arose hurriedly, intending to join the rest and to cut short the hateful conference.   This movement Friar Tuck, who had been peacefully dozing at her feet, misinterpreted to mean a declaration of war upon her enemy, and, starting up with a growl of deep-seated determination, his teeth gleaming, his body tense,—a terrible object in his wrath,—he launched his great bulk forward in a spring at the offender.   Quick as he was, Brock Vyvan, who, the other men having taken leave, had been rather tamely turning over a book of photographs of cathedrals, while Trix was appropriated by Van Loon, was quicker.   Before Tuck could reach his victim, a firm hand was on his collar, and Trix, flying to the rescue, helped to reduce the huge creature to good behavior.

Dead-white, and with chattering teeth, Mr. Carteret Leeds for once parted with his offensive case, and went off babbling his adieus in an abject sort of way.

"I never saw Tuck do such a thing before," said Trix, as Van Loon prepared to follow his friend. "He's as mild as milk in general. Lucky it was that horrid Mr. Leeds."

"Tuck never before had such provocation," said Eleanor in an undertone to her sister, her heart beating fiercely at the remembered insolence.

"You are goin' to Mrs. Bullion's dinner, ain't you?" asked lingering Timothy, whose chains this meeting had newly welded. "I know you are, for she told me so, before she could get me to say I'd come; and you'll give me the cotillion, won't you, at the next Assembly?"

"I don't know if I'm engaged; I'll see," said Trix, darting a look at Vyvan, who remained inanimate. Some fine lady of his acquaintance had sent him a card for the festivity in question, and, an hour before, he had talked eagerly with the girl about going thither for the pleasure of dancing with her. But the glimpse just afforded him into the workings of fashionable life had apparently chilled his enthusiasm for its functions.

"I should keep both you and Mr. Vyvan if we were dining at home," said Eleanor, when Trix also rose to go.

"Mama is alone to-night, and I couldn't stop," Trix answered; "but Mr. Vyvan need not take the long walk home with Tuck and me."

Again she ventured a shy side-glance. This time

a dark red tinge came upon his cheeks and brow. He made no answer, but when they were outside kept with her in the street.

"I said you need not trouble to walk back with me," she repeated, a little more distinctly.

"I heard you, of course, and I have no wish to intrude my company; but if you think I am going to lose you from my sight till you are within your own front door, you are mistaken. That is n't the way we treat ladies in our part of the world."

"If you don't, you *all but* engage them to dance the cotillion with you, and then leave them in the lurch, to be snapped up by any goose."

"Do you think he is a goose?" he cried, with a joyous tremor in his voice. "Then I will dance with or without you for a week."

"This is 'tew ridic'lous,'" Trix said, trying to turn off her consciousness of pleasure with a jest. "That 's what the backwoodsman remarked when he came home after an Indian raid, and found his home burnt, and his wife and children lying scalped upon the ground."

"Oh, you may laugh at me," he said, now close beside her, the big dog "padding" on the chain ahead, "but I 've been told—I know what 's expected. Half the girls I meet out ask me if I think you 'll marry Mr. Timothy Van Loon. It 's part of the stock conversation of polite society."

"Let us talk about foot-ball," said Trix, mischievously.

ELEANOR, in the hands of her maid, making ready for a dinner, one of the series in honor of their nuptials to which the young couple had not ceased to be bidden, was vexed at her own longing to hear Jerry's foot upon the stairs. He was unusually late, and now there would be no opportunity till they should be in the carriage to pour forth her full soul about the attempted poison of Mr. Carteret Leeds' discourse. She had already made up her mind that malice was at the bottom of it, and she longed, in Jerry's arms, to rid herself of the recollection of a momentary pang of doubt of him. But there was ever a lurking wonder as to who could be the woman the world of gossip had a right to call Jerry's "old flame." Why had she heard of this person, now, for the first time? Then Eleanor laughed at herself for supposing her beautiful Jerry could have gone so far through his young manhood without some aspersion of the sort. In another wife, she would have been first to judge such weakness beneath contempt.

All the same, when she saw the gown Elsa had laid out for her,—a "creation" in reds and watermelon pinks that Gerald had decried,—with some petulance she ordered it away. In its place she put on a robe of black gauze, that should bring out the dazzling freshness of her skin, and serve as a background for the luster of Jerry's diamonds scattered upon her bodice and in her hair. Until now the girl had decked herself, as flowers unfold their petals to the sun, in fragrant unconsciousness of the law that bids them open. Tasting the fruit of knowledge, she had already learned what men of Gerald's stamp make of vital importance in woman's eyes, and then deride them for considering. Gazing at her image in the mirror, and admitting with a blush the success of her

innocent design, the young wife's eye fell on the face
of a tiny clock standing among the litter of silver and
ivory upon her toilet.

"How late it is!" she exclaimed. "You are quite
sure, Elsa, Mr. Vernon has not come into his room?"

The discreet Elsa, tripping away, returned without
bearing comfort; and just as Eleanor began to feel
anxiety succeeding blankness, Jerry's key was heard
in the door below.

"All right; I'm late, but I'll make all the haste I
can," he said, looking in on her for a moment. "Why,
what a swell you are, with your whole jewel-box
emptied over your head and sticking where it fell."

"Is there too much of it — are n't you pleased with
me?" she said, rather cut by his comment.

She had risen, and stood before him in her blooming youth, amid the sparkle of her gems, offering herself to his criticism with a movement half coquettish,
all womanly. Jerry leaned over, and regardless of
Elsa's completed masterpiece, clasped her in his arms,
kissing her lips and cheeks.

"Oh, please go," she said; "you will never have
time to change. The carriage is there now; it is dis-
graceful to be so late."

But when, shrouded by her maid in a long wrap
whose high collar of fur caressed the coils of her nut-
brown hair, and armed with her scepter of curling
ostrich plumes, she sat beside Jerry in the brougham,
and they were driven, at speed, through the lighted
streets, Nell nestled toward him lovingly.

"How unnecessarily fast Beacon drives, Jerry.
I'm sure we have time enough. If Mrs. Van Loon

"ARE N'T YOU PLEASED WITH ME?"

9

is to be there, we are sure to have to wait the usual
half-hour for her. I have so much to tell you.
I don't see why women so often say they dread the
driving out to dinner, because their husbands are always cross; you are always sweet to me then, Jerry,
and we are so deliciously alone."

"I might as well attempt to get my arm around a
Polar bear, as you in that fluffy overcoat," he said
good-humoredly. "But I always like to do what 's
expected of me—so here goes. Now begin, and put
in as much talk as a woman can crowd into three
quarters of a mile, and I 'll promise not to interrupt."

Eleanor's first impulse had been to pour into her
husband's ear the annoyance contributed to her day's
experience by Mr. Carteret Leeds. But she could not
bring herself to mar the happiness of this brief time
with him snatched from the outer world. She talked
on in her rapid girlish way about the incidents of the
day, the contents of her letters, the callers at her tea-
table.

"Henderson and De Witt hoped you would be up
before they left. They were as amusing as ever, and
then Trix came with Tuck and young Vyvan—oh,
Jerry, that 's a delightful boy. I wish, I wish Trix
and he could—but there 's no use thinking of it, I
suppose."

"If Trix knows what is good for her, she will whistle back Van Loon," said Jerry.

"Jerry! You are not in earnest. My buoyant,
sparkling Trix tied to that man—oh, impossible!"

"Your mother don't think it impossible, and the

rest of the world will call Trix a downright fool if she gets another chance at him and lets him go."

"Mama—poor mama—you know she thinks only of what is best for us," began Eleanor, and stopped in embarrassment.

"When a woman's got a family with as little money to support them as your mother has, she's obliged to take views ahead. People who have lived to her time of life see that, if a fellow's decent, marriages come out about the same in the long run. There's nothing, as men look at it, against Timothy; and if Trix don't snap him up, another woman will."

"Jerry, I can't believe you would hold such sentiments," Eleanor said, drawing away from him a little.

"Because we are spoons on each other, it don't follow that every one else need be," he said, with a careless laugh. "But here's news for you, Nell: my mother, who kept me so late talking about her plans, is to sail in the *Teutonic* on Wednesday next. I got a deck stateroom for her and her maid, and cabled Mrs. Vane-Benson to establish her at Claridge's. She and the doctor have patched up between them that she can't stand the climate of New York in spring. The truth is, Nell, she's got the constitution of a horse, and I suspect there's some tiff under it. I believe she sent for her physician like a woman I heard of, lately, who said, 'Doctor, I want to go abroad. Tell me what's the matter with me.'"

"Then you *were* with your mother, after all?" Eleanor said, forgetting in her satisfaction to make filial comment on Mrs. Vernon's plans.

"With her. What do you mean?" he said, withdrawing his arm. "Did n't I tell you I 've been running about all day, settling her affairs ? "

The brougham drew up before an awning, and they walked along a wide crimson carpet up the steps and into the anteroom, where the maids took Eleanor's wraps, she being conscious of increased enjoyment of the hour. Late as she and Jerry were, the company of eighteen or twenty people waiting in the drawing-room were to be yet called upon to curb their pangs of hunger for Mr. and Mrs. Van Loon.

"It is abominable, that woman," a man said, who was talking with Eleanor during this trying interval. "She 's absolutely no consideration for people's digestions. This is the fifth dinner this season where she's kept me waiting for my food. I 'm faint now, and if I did n't know what this chef can do, I 'd go ask the butler for a sandwich, and accept the consequence. Here they are now, for a wonder — but," his jaw dropped as he looked around him, "by Jove, I 'm an odd number, and there 's another yet to come ! "

As he spoke, a glimpse of somebody hastening in at the door in white and pearls caught Eleanor's eye, as "Mrs. de Lancey" was announced. Then the host assuming possession of the bride to lead a glittering line of couples out to the dining-room, Nell was seated and unbuttoning her gloves before discovering that at the other end of a table set with orchids in silver vases, on the right hand of Jerry, who had taken his hostess out, Hildegarde was placed.

"There is a beauty worth waiting for," said their host to Mrs. Van Loon and Eleanor, directing their attention to the last-comer.

9*

"I don't know," said Mrs. Van Loon, who resented encroachment upon her privilege. "The best thing about her is that one don't have to ask Smithson, now they are divorced. And if I were you," she added to Eleanor, while stabbing at an oyster with her fork as comfortably as if it were the reputation of a friend, "I'd haul my husband over the coals for her delay. Half-past six it was, by the carriage-clock, as I drove by the Plantagenet, where she lives, and saw Mr. Vernon going in with her! Did I tell you I've got you down for my Centennial Minuet? It is going on finely, in spite of the women's fights."

X

N the weeks that followed her first perception of Gerald's intention to falsify his actions to her, Eleanor tried to persuade herself that the fault was on her side in demanding that he should sacrifice for her those pleasures of outside companionship she was so eager to give up for him. With the rest of the unsought knowledge the young woman was daily absorbing, came a relentless conviction of the inherent difference in their natures that made it impossible for him to be happy without perpetual movement, variety, change of occupation. If he had been thrown upon his own exertions for their livelihood, he would have been better balanced in this community, where work is the rule, and an idler is by public opinion forced to herd with a little band of his kind, more or less held in reproach for the gifts of fortune. Jerry would have made a capital man of business. His natural industry, daring spirit, gaiety, quickness of intuition, surface good temper, eminently fitted him to deal with American leaders of affairs. For politics he had little taste, but the whip-and-spur atmosphere

of modern commerce or finance would have suited him thoroughly. Soon after leaving the university, Jerry had showed symptoms of weariness of the vacuity of his life in New York, and, to his mother's dismay, had made a movement to join the ranks of those men noted curiously by aliens to the metropolis — men who, possessing long purses, addict themselves to money-making through heredity, and toil all day in office or counting-room, returning tired at night to houses that are palaces, and to wives better equipped in luxury than are most princesses. Mrs. Vernon, in dread of a return to hated "trade," protested vigorously. And Jerry, who, but for a few thousands a year left him by his father, was dependent upon her for means, was overcome, and contented himself with making time pass merrily, as did the others of his class.

After Eleanor found out that the world — the sharp-tongued world that must have food for talk, and thought it no ill nature to discuss the relations of this conspicuous pair — was openly commenting on her Gerald's early return to his allegiance to Hildegarde, who was neither invited nor petted the less, the young wife ventured upon the common resource of a proud, wounded creature under such circumstances, and went out of her way to include Mrs. de Lancey in their domestic intimacy. Jerry's passionate protests that Eleanor alone had power to sway his love (uttered in their reconciliation after bursts of impatient anger that terrified his wife), that for Mrs. de Lancey he felt only the sympathy all men must feel for a dear sweet woman whose sorrows had made her sacred, that Hildegarde thought Eleanor the most charming, noble, generous being in the world, and valued her friendship beyond all earthly boons— these assurances the wife often hugged to her heart to soothe its aching.

Sometimes, when puzzling over the contradictions of her married lot, Nell felt inclined to ask some one of wider experience if there had been anything her ignorance had left undone in her relation to her husband. She could not speak to her mother, or even to Betty, for that would be to reveal Jerry's deficiencies, and them she would have shielded from her own people until death. It would have been a relief to talk to Jerry's mother, who, whatever her faults of judgment, loved him fervently. But Mrs. Vernon, in the aroma of plutocracy upon its travels, had steamed away in the *Teutonic* weeks before, and was heard of as in the act of establishing herself in Prince's Gate as a householder among the aristocracy of London; and Eleanor had not been long in realizing that intercourse between the son and mother seemed to result rather in pain to both than pleasure to either, and that separation between them was the price of peace.

No; the wings of appeal to the sympathy of fellowbeings must lie folded in a case like this. All that Eleanor prayed for was that her own love for Jerry might not be strained. In silence, in the night, abroad in gay gatherings where a chance word summoned it, this feeling was ever vigilant.

Aunt Tryphena allowed—and Tryphena was a virgin of uncompromising hostility to modern fashionable life—that Jerry had drawn a prize in Eleanor. The colossal lady, who, always at odds with her sister-in-law, lived alone in a great, tasteless house, was accounted queer and stingy, and would take offense when one least expected it, displayed in her way quite a liking for Mrs. Gerald.

"But for that weak-minded, stand-off mother, and the insufferably sharp Betty, and little giggling Trix dragging about that monster of a dog," Miss Tryphena Vernon would aver she considered that "Jerry had done better than Luella Ann had any reason to expect." Nell, delighted at an opportunity to expend a little tenderness upon anything that came to her from Gerald, was kind and forbearing with the cross old woman, but Miss Tryphena was too wont to burst into invective against Gerald's surroundings and pursuits to make her society a thing to be desired.

There was one of Eleanor's friends of girlhood who seemed intuitively to fathom the young wife's embarrassments. Mr. Theobald, who came to her house infrequently, found her one afternoon, after a little difference with Jerry over the luncheon-table, sitting alone with a book in her hand, but her thoughts evidently scattered. He could not deny to himself that her face was more lovely than on the day when, as a bride, she embodied the one passion of his life-time. He wondered, with a sort of fury against Fate, if it could be that those eyes of hers were made so bewilderingly soft by unshed tears. But he sat down, hat in hand, in commonplace fashion, in a three-cornered carved chair, talked of the book she was reading, of pictures in the Spring exhibitions, of a sale of curios, advised her to keep up her French by subscribing for

"OH! I AM GLAD THAT TEMPEST IN A TEA-POT IS OVER."

the "Revue Bleue," and complimented her successful costume in the late Centennial Minuet.

"Oh! I am glad that tempest in a tea-pot is over," said Eleanor, smiling. "They say our ball has set the women and half the men in society at war. Fortunately, my share was limited to allowing Elsa to put on me a 'grandmother's gown' made new for the occasion, and standing up in it like a fraud to dance where Mrs. Van Loon told me to go. You'll believe me when I tell you how tired I am of parties, how I'm wearying for the summer and life out-doors. I always told you that I am a gipsy at heart—in the days when you lent me your copies of 'Lavengro' and the 'Bible in Spain,' don't you remember?"

Did he remember? The staid, conventional man sitting opposite her felt his heart thump at an unjustifiable rate of speed. Theobald made haste to lead the conversation back to its safer channels.

"If you were sovereign, Trix was a formidable rival at the ball," he said. "I could not imagine the little witch would come out such a stunning beauty as she was that night. Everybody has been talking of it."

"Trix is a darling," Eleanor said, affectionately proud. "But, Tony, she's begun to mystify even me, of late. It looks—I don't like to think so, but it looks —as if she means to feed the flame of Timothy with fuel. When I question her, she evades me, laughing and jesting. Oh! I shall owe a grudge, indeed, to the world we live in, if it colors Trix to make her tolerate that man."

"They are making bets at the clubs she'll take him," Theobald said grimly.

"Trix and I have seen less of each other recently," said Eleanor. "I'm afraid I have been more absorbed than I meant to be in my own affairs, and Betty,— Tony, you know Betty as well as I do; you have always had such an influence in 'quieting her down,' as mama says—Betty's such an oyster about herself, —do you think she can't be well?"

"I think you were always one to distress yourself with imaginings about those you love. I remember, when you were a little girl, going once to your mother's house to find you walking up and down the floor hushing a doll to sleep that you said had scarlet-fever, and your eyes filling with real tears as you implored me to make no noise."

"I suppose I am foolish," Eleanor answered, her eyes deepening with the remembrance. How dim and far away that play-time seemed! How clear the present! How vast, how surcharged with realities!

Betty, arriving on the moment, answered their speculations by an appearance of plentiful good spirits.

"I am just from a final meeting of the ball committee," she said gaily. "Such high jinks! Every one was flurried, and we voted every way the cat jumped. The chairman and the treasurer don't speak, and the secretary cried with vexation when she announced a letter from the Bureau of Authorized Charity warning us against Mrs. Calliope Duncombe as an egregious impostor. Mrs. Duncombe was missing, there was a general row, and what conclusion we arrived at I have not yet found out. But I *think* we are certainly pledged to keep the matter out of the newspapers."

"And the 'Fund for Oppressed Wives'?" asked Eleanor.

"What Mrs. Duncombe has got—if she has any—will no doubt be made up quietly out of the pockets of the heads of the committees; and it seems to me we voted the rest, after expenses shall have been paid, to the Baby Hospital. But one comfort is, there won't be very much to give. Oh, it was beautiful!" said naughty Betty Halliday.

"It's lucky summer is at hand to afford you indefatigable workers a rest," said Theobald.

"I don't know what you call rest. Talk, in the intervals of business, to-day, was just like one of those newspaper columns called 'Summer Plans of the Four Hundred.' I was worn out with listening to the trials of people with cottages to rent, and of people who have rented cottages. One really has enough, in the course of time, of the holes in other people's saucepans. And I'm free to say, I don't care a rap whether Mrs. Bullion is going to try Bar Harbor, or whether Hilda de Lancey has taken that tiny box of the Willie Witherells' at Newport. Nell, you are actually pale; it is this warmish weather, and that bunch of heliotrope too near. Tony, put it away, and open another window, please."

"Thank you," said Eleanor, attempting to smile. "I told Tony just now, I am wearying for the open."

"Has Jerry told you when you are to sail?"

"No—it is not settled; he has not decided," Eleanor answered, her mouth quivering a little.

"Not Newport, I hope? I thought there was no doubt of your summer of roaming in Switzerland. It is just what you need; you have talked of it so long," said Betty in a vexed tone. "Tony, do help me to make this pair of weathercocks decide on their plans."

"You show the influence of your meeting of 'Oppressed Wives,'" said Theobald, rousing a little, to shake off a sort of apathy. "Perhaps, if there's time, you'll both come with me now to the gallery where they've that picture I was just telling Nell about,— the swan-song of a young artist who died on the threshold of his fame,—and you must, of course, see the 'Carmencita,' an astonishing piece of execution. Some one calls Sargent the Paganini of modern painters. Come, Nell; a walk will do you good."

It was like old times, this hurrying on her bonnet, and setting out between Betty and Theobald to look at pictures; and Eleanor enjoyed it. They strolled down the avenue leisurely, the soft air of May inclining them to indolence, and the brightly tinted groups of saunterers offering amusement to the eye. Within the gallery, they paused for a while before the dazzling "Carmencita," and then went back to a frame shrouded in black, with a tablet to show the name of the artist and dates of his birth and recent death.

"Surf and Fog" was the title. Billows crowned with foam rolling in at the feet of the looker-on, the sun, a disk of orange, striving to burn its way through a veil of sea-fog. Only that; but the power and color and life in it had fixed a masterpiece upon the canvas.

Betty, captured by a bright-eyed little man with hair like a pony's mane, to whose lightest utterance about art she listened with respect, went off to make the round of the gallery. Nell and Theobald, busy in con-

versation which had drifted back into their old un-
trammeled familiarity, wandered on till they paused
before a breezy bit of landscape called " Grouse-Cover,"
and there remained, waiting for Betty to find them
out.

Neither noticed that they were the objects of scru-
tiny from two people who stood back of them, then
abruptly crossed in front of Eleanor, and went to the
other room.

"Do you bow to that woman, Nell?" asked Theobald, surprised.

"I—my husband has known Major Shafto for a
long time. They were old comrades traveling in the
East," she answered, coloring deeply. The sight of
Mrs. Shafto's face brought to her so much she fain
would have forgotten.

"And that cad, Leeds. When did you give him
the right to speak to you? Have you done anything
to affront him? I should like to kick the little beggar
for the way he glowered at you out of those mean
eyes of his."

"Oh, Tony, I will tell you. He thinks I set Friar
Tuck on him." And, half-laughing, she gave him a
recital of the episode with Trix's big St. Bernard.

"It served him exactly right, and Tuck should be
awarded a new collar for his good judgment. But it
made Leeds ridiculous, and humbled his enormous
vanity, so I am not surprised at his vengeful look.
Keep out of his way, Nell—that fellow would stoop
to anything; and I may as well put you on your guard
about Mrs. Shafto. I 've known her always, and in
addition to her other shining qualities she is brim-

10

ful of spites against women. I happen to know that she hates your good mother as the devil hates holy water."

"My instincts have been all against her," Eleanor said, with a sigh. "I wish we had not met those two, to spoil such a pleasant old-timey afternoon as you have given me."

"I have made the circuit," Betty said, rejoining them. "For the last ten minutes Carver has been pointing out to me the beauties of an impressionist landscape where they have upset a mustard pot on the lower part of the canvas, and laid on pink plaster with a trowel up above; and I have sworn it is inspired, and he 's gone home to write it up for his paper. But, on the whole, I must agree with you, Tony; this is a brilliant and creditable show."

Betty was cheerful and kindly; her dark face full of animation; her *pince-nez* did not conceal a sparkle in her eye. Eleanor's fears for her health and spirits must have been figments of a fancy disordered by over-search for hidden motives!

Away from the stir and bustle of the town, its activity made languorous by one of those bursts of heat that so often come to New York in spring, a young man was speeding as fast as the Washington express could carry him—and that went no more rapidly ahead than his eager fancy, released to revel in the thought of a glimpse at home and mother. Brock Vyvan, going off for a two-days' holiday, put away moping thoughts as every station brought him nearer to the one he desired to see—a stopping-place whence a way-train presently would jog him leisurely into a country as green as Eden, and as quiet, too.

The little old station, of which one half was a country "store"; the few, shabby, mud-splashed, slow-speaking loungers who stepped up to greet the sole descending passenger; the store-keeper, who was also station-master, and who saluted Brock sociably, shifting his quid; the two or three negroes who hung about at train-time, looking the epitome of the old South's decay,—as much as the passing traveler generally sees of the South *in transitu*, to prejudge all accordingly,—Brock viewed with forbearing eyes. Passing out to the rear platform, he saw the old buggy coated with red mud, containing a patriarchal negro — attired in a Confederate army-coat, from which the brass buttons had been removed, and wearing an ancient Panama hat — who smiled a toothless welcome, as he controlled the quivering pair, Flash and Starlight, that Brock's own hand had broken to harness. The young man stopped to caress his beauties, and to fancy them in Park array, drawing some shining vehicle with rubber tires over perfect roads. If they lacked proper grooming to bring their coats to satin, it was because old Enos had been at work in the field since "sun-up."

Putting his portmanteau into the trap, the young man sprang up beside Enos, and took the reins. Obedient to his voice, the horses went forward with a bound, coming down, despite themselves, ere long, to a snail's speed through mire sometimes hub-deep in holes.

"You 'll have to be a mite keerful here, honey," the

old negro said, as they plunged down a steep incline to a valley where a yellow current rioted, sweeping their way from sight. "'Pears like I disremember ever seein' Goose Crik git up so high. It was for fear of her gittin' wet, I done 'suaded Miss not to come to de deepo to meet you. You knows de best crossin', Marse Brockenbro'—close 'long o' dem stakes. Hol' in Starlight, suh; dat filly 's kind o' feared o' water to dis day."

"Look out for my bag," called Brock, and in a minute they were in the midst of the fierce little river, battling smartly against its rush, the water rising in mid-stream to the horses' necks, and washing to the seat, where the two men had gathered themselves up into a bunch.

"Dat ar little fresh' save me a-cleanin' off de buggy," grinned Enos, when they emerged dripping on the farther side.

Brock's spirits rose. He knew every nook and dingle of the flower-besprinkled woods, every landmark of the rich farming country forsaken by modern enterprise. Beguiling the way with the old negro's talk about plantation and quarter incidents, he, in turn, brought many a stare of wonderment to Enos's eyes by chance disclosures of the scale of New York's magnificence in things of every day. It was when they finally pulled up at a venerable gate, which Enos scrambled down to open, that the patriarch lost a little of his sprightliness.

"You mout take de lower road to de Gret Hus, suh," he said. "It 's easier on de hosses."

"It 's a good mile longer, you old humbug," answered Brock, looking over-head and before him into the green arcade, filtered with sunshine, and sentineled with boles of ancient trees. These woods were to be his own, and of their witchery nothing he had ever seen elsewhere had robbed them. He had his way, and followed the customary road leading to the house, until ringing sounds of the axes of busy woodcutters made him rein in the horses shortly.

"What 's that, old man?" he asked, a frown coming upon his face.

"Oh, Marse Brockenbro', suh," Enos said mournfully, "it was 'cause o' dis I was wantin' you to go de udder way, an' let Miss hab de breakin' o' de news. Old Marse has done tuk a contrac' to supply de new railroad wid ties, suh, what 's goin' to run nigh heah. Farmin' 's powerful po' down dis a-way, an' we ain' been flourishin'—we needs de money mightily, Marse Brockenbro'."

"That 'll do. Don't say any more about it," Brock answered, biting his lip. He drove through the hollow in which the men were at work, and vouchsafed not a glance at the clearings where unwonted sunlight peered into nature's hiding-place for a lush growth of ferns and mosses. The piles of wood, already cut and stacked, seemed to him so many funeral pyres for the sacrifice of things beloved and reverenced. When they had gained the higher land beyond, and were trotting briskly along under a forest archway, his quick eyes saw at the end of it, waiting by the roadside beneath a huge old cherry-tree, lately a pyramid

10*

of bloom, a tall figure clothed in black, at her side a couple of hounds, and a hearth-bred lamb that followed like a dog.

Brock uttered a boyish shout as his mother waved her hand. She was in his arms, and the trap sent forward, a moment later. There was no frown left upon his brow as they strolled toward the house, her thinner blood pulsing a glad answer to the rich current in his young veins. In the perfectness of love between these two was to be found the religion of Vyvan's life.

THE old dwelling of Mount St. Dunstan stood near the summit of a hill crowned with an orchard, its famous gardens sheltered from the wind. Farther down the slope were the quaint colonial stables where tradition said many grandees of early American society had sent their steeds (which must have been giraffes) to be tied under racks suspended high upon the walls, while their masters enjoyed the good cheer of the mansion-house. Here Enos, who was already engaged in unharnessing Flash and Starlight, looked from Brock to his mistress with an imploring gaze, as the young man paused at the stable door.

"One minute, mother, till I've had a peep at Houpla," he said.

"Brockenborough—my dear boy," she answered, holding his hand within her own, "I hoped you would wait till to-morrow. We have sold the colt to Rhynders for a gentleman in Washington, at a price we could not afford to refuse."

Brock's lips were compressed, but he said nothing.

He could not bear to visit the empty stall, and, squeezing his mother's hand, he walked on with her past the house to the terrace above, and stopped by a moss-grown sun-dial to look back.

Built of substantial brick trimmed with white stone, the two advancing wings to the house formed a central court where the turf grew fine and soft over vaulted cellars beneath. Tall old trees stroked the hipped roof with their branches, and ivy, long unpruned, curtained the walls. Pigeons wheeling and circling in the air, a collection of dogs of assorted breeds and values, the distant view of wagons following a farm-road from the fields, the sound of negroes singing or whistling — all served to relieve the almost somber influence of the scene.

"We shall find him in the garden," said Mrs. Vyvan's low voice, breaking Brock's reverie. "You will be glad to see your dear grandfather so wonderfully well. The spring, when he can live out of doors, seems to bring him a new lease of life."

They passed through a turnstile set in a hedge of box, and lo! they were in a fairy-land of bloom. Fled away were the young man's thoughts of sorrow. The declining sunlight here lay cradled on verdant spaces of turf, alternating with flower-beds of ancient pattern aglow with fragrant color. Leaning over a plot of late-blooming tulips, the aged master of Mount St. Dunstan was descried, his familiar, the golden collie, swept by his faded coat-tails.

"Brockenbro', my dear boy, you are welcome home," the old man said in a reedy voice, his blue eyes filled with merry twinkles. "Just look at my tulips, will you? It's the first year I've made 'em jostle the roses. Ah, building houses to last for all time is very well for you, sir, but give me the planting of flowers that come fresh every season, and that have a thousand freaks of beauty you can never count upon."

It was no wonder the county was proud of old Mr. Octavius Brockenborough, his grandson fondly thought, while surveying the lines of the cameo-face, the long silver locks that fell upon his slightly stooped shoulders, the genial kindness of his smile. Eighty-four, and the survivor of a once numerous and influential family, his sons had dropped away before him, and of his daughters, married and scattered, only Mrs. Vyvan, the youngest of his children, had presented him with a descendant. "A fine type — a fine specimen of our best old stock," his neighbors would say on the rare occasions when the old gentleman showed himself in public, at church, or court-house. "No business sense," they would add reluctantly. "Never had any idea of holding on to his money, or of running his farms to pay. And, to sum all up, he's been giving, and putting his name to notes, and letting dead-beats prey on him, all his life. And that's what's become of the fine Brockenborough property, once as good as any in the State."

There was no pinch of fortune visible in the old man's face to-day, as he led Brock hither and thither among his darlings, showing their various perfections and shielding their defects. The young fellow could not help thinking how somebody he knew would like to patter about these blossomy walks, and listen to their kind old master's talk. How it would make her

"YES; IT IS TOO BAD."

laugh—one of those hearty, ringing peals—to see all of the dogs, save Colin Clout, the privileged, stand in a ring around the turnstile, eying the insider with abject envy!

When Mrs. Vyvan, with her store-room keys and her pet lamb, had betaken herself away on supper thoughts intent, the old man led his grandson in-doors to the best parlor, where, throwing back the shutters, he admitted the full light.

"You'll be sorry to see dampness has played the mischief with the Vandyck," he said, pointing to a portrait in a tarnished frame hanging above the chimneypiece—a cavalier in court-dress, whose lip and cheek were overspread by a stain like a lichen upon a stone.

"Yes; it is too bad," went on old Octavius, answering his grandson's comment. "But I believe your mother has been writing to an artist in New York, who will come down to set it straight when we can raise the money to send for him. What'll ye think, Brockie, my boy, of a Senator's wife in Washington, who'd heard of our pictures, sending me an offer for the Vandyck? Well, well, they and the land and the books are about all we've got left. Those two portraits Woolaston painted of my father and mother— no great value as works of art, perhaps, but I'm fond of them. And my Aunt Dolly, in hunting costume, yonder, over the door, was married in the very spot where you're standing. Dead and gone all! Such a fine frolic as we had—I was a boy of nineteen, and, during the week of merry-making over her wedding, danced out a pair of pumps. The house full, and the neighbors' houses full, plenty of wine in our cellars, and the stalls of the stables filled—heigh-ho! Did I tell ye, boy, when the locust-tree blew down a month ago, we found upon one branch nests of half a dozen different kinds of birds? Recently your mother was troubled by bees in her pantry-window, and we could find no trace of 'em. At last old Tom took off a plank or two of the clapboarding outside, and, by George! sir, he got five pounds o' delicious honey up under the eaves. And I 've laid hands on the Camerarius Plautus you wanted,—it was tucked away on the shelf with the 'Sporting Magazines,' where you left it yourself, you rascal—meant to send it by express, but it passed out o' my mind, there 's so much to do, and so much going on —"

With the old man's voice in his ears, Brock stepped out of the moldering room full of phantoms of long-gone solvency. In the corridor beyond they found an aged negress, tidily dressed, and bobbing droll courtesies to the gentlemen.

"Dilsey, what you want, girl?" said old Octavius. "Why, Brockie, it 's you Aunt Dilsey has come in to see, of course."

"Sarvant, marsters, hopin' you 's well. I 's uncommon po'ly, thank de Lawd. I des drapped in to pay my respecks to Marse Brockenbro', en brung him two guinea-eggs for his brekfus. Ain't you got no news to tell de plantation folks, Marse Brockie, 'bout some mighty rich lady what we 's spectin' you to git married to, so 's to fotch de old Moun' St. Duns'n times back ag'in?"

"No news, Aunt Dilsey," Brock answered, trying

to smile; but the question hit him hard. When, before bedtime, at an hour they had always chosen for mutual confidence, the mother and son were alone together, he sternly put away the desire to tell her of his bewitchment. He even repressed the intended request to his grandfather for a box of the "rarest, fairest" of Mount St. Dunstan roses, to take back to "a friend who had been kind" to him in New York.

XI

"Y dear Trix," said Miss Halliday to her younger sister, one June morning when they were sitting together in their second-story room looking into the Square,—Trix, with her "Promessi Sposi" and dictionary, Betty, who had been writing the usual notes, emerging from a darkling reverie,—"you may as well pay attention, for I 'm about to be hateful."

"Don't bring me back to things of every day, please. Here am I doing my best to forget my gnawing anxiety as to Jack's getting into the boat. I think it 's positive cruelty to animals to keep the men—and their sisters—waiting on the anxious bench this way, and never to know till the last minute whether he is going to row in the race or not."

"I have a vague idea the universe will keep on about the same if Jack does n't row this year. There are matters more important nearer home, my dear. I wonder if you know how abominably poor we are."

"I 've heard it ever since I could think," said Trix, carelessly. "Everybody in New York who is n't rich is abominably poor."

"It has come to a crisis, now."

"I thought so, when the stair-carpet is so worn it is n't worth sending to be cleaned again; and our dinners,—it 's a mercy, with my appetite, that we 're invited out so much,—and I really don't know how I 'm clothed. I 'm quite aware that in spite of our dear little mummy's plotting and piecing to turn me out a credit to the family, I never am equipped from head to foot like other girls. When I get a good jacket, there 's no skirt to wear with it, and my winter hats have to go with spring costumes. Just think of Nell, Betty — what richness! Mama was very liberal with her trousseau, and Jerry has made her buy such a lot more. Nell wanted to give me her new marron cloth that just came home; but I would n't hear of it — would you ?"

"No, certainly. Let us be independent of wealthy brothers-in-law, or perish. But do you know what the mother has gone to her lawyer's again this morning for ?"

"Something about that mortgage, that 's like Poe's raven on our door, I suppose. It 's been there forever, but we still keep along."

"She 's been eating up her capital for five years past, and thought she could hold out, poor dear, until you — I 'm hopeless, and don't count."

"Until I — what have I got to do with eating capital ?"

"Till you follow Nell's example, and supply yourself with a somebody to give you such an establishment as mother thinks a Halliday girl should have."

"I don't know why a Halliday girl should n't be

easy her own way," said Trix, still lightly, but sitting more erect and looking more womanlike.

"That's mother's weakness, and she's had it so long we can't alter matters now," went on Betty, persistently. "She—she asked me to have this talk with you. She thinks we have kept you long enough in ignorance of the real state of affairs. There's been an offer to buy the house."

"This house—my father's house!" said Trix.

"It is too big for ordinary people, and would cost immensely to do over in modern fashion. But the —— Club has had an eye on it for a long time, it seems, and mother got their offer yesterday."

"She will never accept it!" protested Trix.

"The money would free her from a load of care, and pay Jack's way through college, and—oh, a hundred things."

"It would break Jack's heart to sell this house. We have always planned how he is to live here with his wife,—at least I have,—and I could see Jack was pleased."

"Jack, like the rest of us, will have to submit to common sense. Of course the matter won't be decided immediately, but mother thought you ought to know; and, Trix, I believe she wants, too, to warn you a little —against—we see what outsiders do not, of course —how much is depending upon you."

The smooth-spoken Betty was actually hesitating, nonplussed for proper words. Trix, with the impulse of a colt in a paddock, wanted to shy off and gallop away to the other end of it.

"I don't know—yes, I won't tell a lie, I do know

what you mean," she said suddenly, turning scarlet.
" But you may just tell mama she 's no cause to warn
me,— I have n't been running the risks she fears,—it
is n't likely I 'll go after a man who don't want me.
And if he did, does n't every soul I know tell me that
to marry a young professional man in New York is
putting a clog on him that holds him back? Who
wants to hold anybody back?" our Trix ended, dan-
gerously near to tears.

"It was n't only that," Betty said, for her, wretchedly embarrassed. "People have been talking to her
a good deal about the encouragement you 're supposed
to be giving Timothy Van Loon —"

"O girls, how good to find you in here and alone!"
cried Eleanor, who, interrupting Betty, saved her from
a stormy answer. While they gave her glad welcome,
Nell's sisters read in her face traces of recent disquie-
tude. It had not taken long for the young wife's
family to find out that her life was not all on velvet,
and they had wisely agreed to invite no confidences.
And so Mrs. Gerald's entrance, preceded by old Andrews, who had never walked before Nell Halliday up
to the second floor, had about it just the right amount
of flutter and importance the movements of the brilliantly successful member of the family should have.
Betty got up to meet her, and Trix gave her the best
arm-chair, sitting down on a stool at her feet prepared
to admire indiscriminately all that Eleanor said, or
did, or wore. And old Norah, arriving in a clean cap
and apron, hovered in the background, casting fond
looks upon her former nursling.

"You dear thing, how good of you to come!" said

11

Trix, hugging her sister's knees. "You 're just in time to prevent Betty and me from squabbling."

But she took care not to tell the subject of their difference, nor was Mrs. Gerald Vernon admitted into the family discussion about what Betty called their "crisis." It was tacitly understood among them that no possible representation should be made to Eleanor that might seem to appeal for aid from Eleanor's husband. Until and after the arrival of their mother, pale and jaded, from her expedition down-town, the talk was as cheerful as the sisters three could make it. Trix could not but note how, in gazing at her comfortable, smartly dressed daughter, whose carriage and footman stopped the way, Mrs. Halliday's face relaxed from its lines of settled care.

Before Nell arose to go, it was clear she had something particular to say. Her sisters, who knew every expression of her candid face, watched a blush come into it as she divulged the object of her call.

"Jerry has made a plan. He says all the boating-men think there is no doubt Jack will be on the Yale crew. And in any case it will be a treat to Trix —"

"Don't say to go up to New London for the race, or I shall lose my senses with delight!" ejaculated Trix.

"Yes; he thinks we shall all enjoy it — mama and Betty too."

"Count me out," said Mrs. Halliday, promptly. "I could n't bear to see my poor dear boy strain himself in any such dreadful way. And if he don't get 'on,' he 'll be so blue I had rather not be with him."

"I had," said Trix. "Jack will need me, in any

event. And if Jerry knew how I've been turning over in my mind every respectable way of getting to New London for that day—oh, he's a perfect dear to have thought of it!"

"He had already talked of it to me," went on Eleanor, visibly embarrassed, "and I was planning a surprise for Trix. And then, it appears, Jerry found out that Mr. Van Loon considered *us* engaged to go up for the Yale-Harvard race in his new yacht, the *Incognita*."

"So we are to meet you there?" exclaimed Trix, beaming. "That's not quite so good as going with you, dear, but still—"

"No; Mr. Van Loon asks Jerry to—ask mama,—he wants you both to come on the yacht,—and if mama won't go, he thought you would be satisfied to be chaperoned by me—"

"I like being chaperoned by you," said Betty, to bridge over the awkward silence and the effect of Trix's altered face. "You will find me such a giddy little thing!"

"I am awfully sorry," Eleanor went on. "I said everything I could to Jerry; but he feels bound,—you know men are so punctilious about engagements with each other—are they not, mama? He says he really couldn't consent to throw over Mr. Van Loon; and the trip is a short one—we needn't be on the yacht more than three days. Mama, tell Betty and Trix whether you want them to go or not, and we'll all abide by you."

Poor Mrs. Halliday's eye at that moment lighted upon a pigeonhole in her desk that she knew to be full of unpaid bills. The talk with her lawyer had sent her home with a driven feeling. The big house they lived in could not be maintained upon air. If they sold it, the mortgage would absorb all but enough of the purchase-money to give her a pittance of additional income. By the necessity for keeping appearances up to the mark of gentility in New York of the present day, she had to acknowledge herself badly beaten. And, now, by shifting her gaze she could again see the reassuring spectacle of Eleanor's carriage and Eleanor's servants in the street. Only that morning she had made some excuse to old Andrews in telling him that he must leave her service.

"I think when Jerry and Eleanor are so much put out about it, you had better make no difficulties, girls," she said vaguely, her tongue dry in her mouth.

"You will go? It is settled," said Eleanor, rather hurrying the thing. "I shall tell Jerry. It will please him so much, you can't think. I shall take care that the whole affair is made pleasant; I believe I can promise that—"

"Are we to be the only women on board for the race?" asked Betty, Trix remaining obstinately glum.

"Oh, I think so, certainly," said Eleanor. "It is my party, Jerry says. There will be another man or two, of course. But, dear me! it is nearly a quarter past, and I'm due at Fiftieth street at half past one. Good-by, and come to me soon to lunch or dinner. Good-by, mammy darling. I have had such a mean little glimpse of you. Oh, I must n't forget to tell you it is settled we 're to sail about the middle of July."

With Eleanor, Trix also vanished from the room.

"Jerry meant Nell to bring us into this," said Betty to her mother. "That is the reason I made no spoken objection. I should n't be surprised if our consent were the price she pays for getting him to say they will positively sail."

"Jerry is an only son, and accustomed to domineer a little over women. I can't understand why he has wavered about their plans. Nell will be happier traveling with him, and it has always been intended they should spend this summer in England and Switzerland, and the autumn in the East," said Mrs. Halliday, dwelling comfortably upon schemes for her favorite child that involved such liberal expense.

"I won't tell mama," thought Betty, "that everybody says Jerry 's completely in the toils of Hildegarde again, and that is the reason he wants to make Timothy secure with Trix."

"It 's all one to me, mother," she said, with a whimsical attempt at gaiety. "But this much you must understand. I 've had my talk with Trix, and I felt like a sneak-thief all the time. If it were anybody but that—Timothy Van Loon—"

"Who a month or so ago was ready to marry another woman if she would throw her handkerchief to him, and was driven off the field by Jerry's occupation of it," was what passed through her mind—to be suppressed.

"Every one says Mr. Van Loon is a devoted son," ventured poor Mrs. Halliday, forlornly. "And our families have long been allied—since his great-grandaunt married your father's great-uncle's brother-in-law. It has always been considered a safe family,"

11*

she added; and Betty, wrung with sudden pity, bent down and kissed her mother's brow.

"As if any one were satisfied with married life — or gets exactly what she wants!" she meditated, further, in her room. "If I had even a medium-sized purse, I'd begin to think a spinster's lot the only 'happy one.'"

ONE beautiful moonlight night in the end of June saw Mr. Van Loon's much paragraphed new yacht, the *Incognita*, steal away from her moorings near the foot of —— street on the East River, and glide in a ghostly manner out into the Sound. On her deck was a small, not particularly well assorted party of guests, consisting of Mr. and Mrs. Gerald Vernon, Betty and Beatrix Halliday, a couple of club-men, hangers-on of Timothy, a new Swedish attaché in process of illumination about the States, and the owner of the boat. Down in the women's cabins, with their wondrous modern upholstery and brass beds, Elsa was engaged in laying out her ladies' belongings for the night, as if it were some country-house at which they had arrived for a three-days' visit.

Van Loon, in naval blue, and with gold-laced cap, treading his own deck by moonlight, Betty decided to be Van Loon at his best. He did not obtrude his attentions upon Trix, and yet somehow she, and every one else, was made to feel that this floating fairy palace under the snowy sails was waiting that lucky young woman's nod to dip its colors into her keeping. "Oh, if it were always moonlight on a yacht, and Timothy were always thus subdued!" Betty wanted to whisper in her sister's ear, yet dared not. The next day found them at anchor off the far-famed hostelry known as the Pequot House, near the staid old town of New London, where on the morrow the annual race between Yale and Harvard was to be won and lost. Electing to go ashore, the ladies found themselves at once in the merry turmoil of Regatta week. The halls and verandas of the hotel were thronged with brilliantly dressed women — mothers, sisters, sweethearts, and general admirers of the rival crews. Collegians from both universities swarmed in attendance on their fair, but the handsome young Harvard men seemed to predominate in numbers.

Trix, upon landing, began to look about her for somebody to whom she might confide her growing emotions about the question of the hour. To be so near her brother Jack,— now, without dispute, exalted to be an actual member of the great Yale crew, and about, for the honor of his university, to row at Number 2,— and to hold no intercourse with him, not even to hear how he was passing these last trying days in that mysterious stronghold up yonder at Gale's Ferry, tantalized her cruelly. It was absolutely of no use, the girl had made up her mind, to expect the right sort of sympathy aboard the yacht. Jerry and Van Loon were Harvard graduates; Nell basely took sides with her husband; Betty made fun of everything; the other men aboard had no bias either way. Among the numbers of people encountered at the Pequot, it was her ill fortune to know only those who claimed Van Loon and Nell and Jerry as sympathizers with the crimson.

It was, therefore, with a throb of keen joy that she beheld Mr. Brock Vyvan, with a knot of dark-blue ribbon in the buttonhole of his neat tweed coat, and a band of dark-blue ribbon around his straw hat, walking up and down the veranda in attendance upon a mother and daughter, the latter vivacious and pretty enough to give Trix a sober second thought. Her first impulse was to thrust herself upon young Vyvan's attention, to lean forward, to fix him with a bow and smile that should be followed up at his earliest convenience by his adjournment to her side. The next moment Trix drew back, and hid herself behind her sister Nell, in a blaze of color at her own indiscretion. Mr. Vyvan had indeed seen her, had bowed with the rather pronounced courtesy of the Southerner—but he had not smiled. Trix fancied he did not want to avail himself of her implied permission. What—oh, dreadful thought!—if he wanted to rebuke her forwardness?

The gala-day was darkened after that. The Van Loon party, observed of all, passed up and down the promenade; the ladies had taken their cups of tea, and were about to return aboard, when Trix fell in with a young woman she had known casually in town, and had ignored hitherto—a plain girl, with no especial points to praise or to decry. At this juncture, if she had had, in girls' language, "every hair of her head strung with diamonds," Trix could not have valued the plain girl more. For she wore a tarpaulin hat with a broad blue band, and five minutes' conversation developed the fact that she owned a cousin on *the* crew. Eager as Trix was to ask was she to answer. The very latest news from Gale's Ferry was hers, thanks to an undergraduate brother, who had brought word that their men were as "fit as fiddles" and "regularly smooth."

"Thank Heaven!" Trix said, kissing the plain girl fervently. In the relief of the moment she almost forgot Mr. Brock Vyvan. "You see, I don't know a single Yale person here to ask," she explained.

"There are plenty, and the very nicest," answered the plain girl, bridling. To which Trix answered: "Oh, of *course!* I shall know *thousands* of them to-morrow," and kissed her new-old friend again.

When they walked down to the wharf to get into the yacht's boat, she ahead with Timothy, Beatrix again saw Mr. Brock Vyvan—a back view only. He had parted company with the pretty girl and her mama, and was striding away as if shod with seven-league boots. She did not see him turn, after their own little party was embarked, and gaze over at the *Incognita*, lying at anchor and flying under her official colors a crimson flag.

"Blank him! I should like to strangle him," murmured this peaceful young Vyvan.

Gerald, after dining on the yacht, went ashore for the dance, as did the other men, the women preferring to save themselves for the excitement of the morrow. But they were not without a visitor. A small boat, coming alongside, sent up a dapper youth, who presented himself, following his card, as a reporter for a New York daily newspaper.

"I will not intrude on you, ladies, for more than a moment," he said in a businesslike manner. "I merely wanted to ask if Mrs. Gerald Vernon, as an exponent of the Four Hundred of New York, would object to giving 'The Planet' her opinion of the Bob Cook stroke."

"My opinion?" gasped Eleanor, fairly astonished. "Why, I have n't any. And if I had, what possible value or interest could it have to the editor or readers of 'The Planet'?"

"It is a special thing, gotten-up for the issue of our paper that announces the result of the race," he said, unabashed. "We think ladies should have a voice in every question, nowadays, and I have quite a list of society leaders known to be visiting New London to interview."

"You must excuse me," said Eleanor, and, bowing and smiling, the dapper man, who had no time to lose, took himself away to glean in more remunerative fields.

And now the day has dawned that is to crown and quench so many hopes on the New World Thames. Bright and early the yacht, flying every pennant and oriflamme on board, waits orders to push ahead to follow the race, to be rowed at eleven, down-stream. A smart little breeze is blowing, and the choppy sea causes the yacht's boat, returning from the hotel, to dance up and down merrily, to the excitement of her cargo of womenkind.

For, to the strong disgust of Eleanor and Betty,— Trix just now is above details,—Gerald has announced to them that Mr. Van Loon, having met Major and Mrs. Shafto and their party at the Pequot dance, could

not get out of inviting them to pass the day on the
Incognita to see the race. Who makes up the party,
Eleanor does not ask, or Jerry say. All too soon there
arrive Miss Kitty Foote, the vague young Foote her
brother, Mr. Carteret Leeds, and—Mrs. de Lancey!

"And I shall expect you to be civil to these women,"
ends Jerry, remonstrating against his wife's too plain
distaste. "I don't want your offish ways with them,
any more than Betty's infernal spitefulness."

"But, Jerry, you gave us no idea—"

"Who had an idea?" he answered, his face flushing.
"Nell, if I were you, I should try to bear in mind that,
however much he loves his wife, no man can stand
petty jealousies and heavenly superiority. No man, I
say."

"I make neither charge nor assumption," Nell replied, fronting him haughtily.

"Oh! I know what a jealous woman is. Suppose I
were such a goose about Theobald?"

"Theobald?" she repeated faintly.

"Yes. Do you imagine people have n't tried to put
it into my head that he's still in love with you? Now,
I 've no time to say more, for here they are; but mind
what I have said."

"O Gerald!" her pale lips syllabled. The next moment this bit of tragedy of every day is crushed out
of sight; the young couple are advancing from where
they had walked aside for a brief conjugal talk, and are
greeting the newcomers as if nothing had occurred.

OVER the course steams the little white launch *Yale*,
bearing the referee with the unwelcome tidings that

because the water is so rough the race has been postponed till six P. M., and is to be rowed up-stream instead of down. While the party on the *Incognita*, and other pleasure crafts lying around them in the stream below the Shore Line Bridge, solace themselves with luncheon and the popping of champagne-corks, steamboats, tugs, sloops, every variety of water-vehicle, go hither and thither in vexed confusion.

Trix, who has nerved herself with real heroism to bear the delay, makes an excuse to leave the cabin, and goes again on deck. With her blue silk shirt belted around her slim, maidenly waist, her close-fitting blue serge skirt, her white straw sailor-hat with the blue band and bit of white tulle tied across her bright eyes and blooming cheeks, she presents a captivating image of fidelity to Yale. In vain had Timothy tempted her with a bunch of Jacqueminot roses supplied by his steward from the unromantic ice-box. She had almost stamped her foot at him as she waved the insidious crimson beauties off. Oh, for one who has the impulse and the thought to give her a little posy of Yale *bleuets* to wear on her loyal breast! But there is none, not one in that band of jesting folk around the long cabin-table a-glitter with glass and silver, to understand the yearning of her heart! As she walks out toward the railing, and strains her eyes in the direction of the crew's quarters, and longs to have speech with Jack, dear, eager Jack, who must be suffering so cruelly with the delay, a step is heard behind her, and she turns to confront little Mr. Foote, exquisite in a costume invented for the day.

"I'm going ashaw for an hour," he said.   "A little business at the Crockaw House."

A drowning man in his extremity is said to clutch at a straw, and into Trix's wilful head pops the idea of utilizing Mr. Foote.

"Would it trouble you very much to drop me at a friend's house in the town?" she asked, oh, so sweetly!—"and to pick me up on your way back to the yacht?"

"Delighted, I'm shaw," said the flattered youth, never doubting that her plan was prearranged.

Trix pencils a note to her sisters, and without delay descends into the boat in waiting to take off Mr. Foote.   She has a delicious sense of escape from bondage, a childish tremor lest she be overtaken and called back.   It is her purpose to repair to the home of a certain kindly matron, an old friend of her mother's, who is sure to have a houseful of wearers of the blue, and in a half-hour's chat relieve herself of some of the pent-up emotion of the day.   Nell and Betty certainly can't take her to task for the civility of a call on Mrs. Mordant, who had invited her for the whole Regatta week.

XII

OING ashore, Trix and her trim little escort crossed the railway-track, and were at once in a cloud of blue jackets, coaches, and old Yale oarsmen who had come down to town to get the latest quotation of the betting, and, by a dip into that excitement, strive to escape the awful hush that hung over the quarters of the crew. In the confusion, Trix saw Vyvan chatting with a Goliath in flannels on the sidewalk just ahead, and the hats of both men flew off as she came abreast of them. Something in the atmosphere of common sympathy made her ignore her fears of the day before. She cast upon Vyvan a smile so kind, so frank, so fearless, that the young man's resolution melted in thinnest air.

"Miss Halliday," he said, joining her, "may I tell you that I 've just heard from the highest authority that your brother and our other men are bearing up finely, and we need n't be afraid of the strain upon their nerves?"

The delight in her face gave him no hint to be off, and during their walk up the main street of the distractedly gay town little Mr. Foote was left to solace himself by gazing at the display of racing haberdash-

174

ery in the shop-windows on each side of the way. It
was slow progress amid the joyous, expectant throngs,
every step impeded by gangs of college oarsmen and
their followers. The heroes of the crews who had
already that week strutted their brief hour upon the
stage,—of the universities of Pennsylvania, Cornell,
and Columbia,—victors and vanquished, were side by
side. Freshmen, Sophomores, Juniors, Seniors met
for once on an even plane of sympathy, together with
many a grizzled graduate who had left his business
and the cares of middle life in town, and from his
class-reunion in Cambridge or New Haven harked
back to New London to the glories of his youth, as
gaily as the youngest. The women folk appertaining
to all these enthusiasts laughed, chatted, and scrambled in the universal crush. Most of them had been
skirmishing for luncheon in a town taken by surprise,
but there were few complaints of discomfort or scanty
rations.

"Oh! is n't it grand?" Trix said. "And to think
how I was wasting time in that horrid yacht in just
being swell!"

They had come to the Crocker House, the headquar-
ters of betting on the race. Here she saw Mr. Foote
cast an anxious glance after a band of callow youngsters like himself pressing in to give and take odds,
on lines strictly partizan, under the persuasions of
gamblers of more experience. In imagination little
Foote was already stretching out his hand to receive
from the depositing office of the hotel an envelop fat
with winnings, after a victory by Harvard.

"If you are in a hurry, Mr. Foote," said the insidious Beatrix, "I would n't keep you from your business, for the world. I think Mr. Vyvan won't mind taking me the rest of the way to Mrs. Mordant's; and you might call there for me when you are ready to go back."

Foote was off in a flash.

"I hope he has laid in his full stock of. summer trousers," Vyvan observed. "Else I 'm afraid there will be not much left to pay his tailor's bill, to-night."

"Then you think we 'll win?" Trix cried, thrilling.

"What sort of Yale man would I be if I did not?" he answered.

"Oh! Oh! How I *love* to hear you talk!" she said, with reckless enthusiasm. "When I think that I 'm doomed to watch the race through a telescope from the deck of that old yacht, where about every soul will be for the other side, and that Jack, my own boy, who 's shared every thought I 've had for years, will be straining his heart out to win for Yale, how can I bear it?—that 's what I 'd like to know."

"You sha'n't, if I can help it," he said rapidly. "See here, Miss Halliday. I don't know what New York girls think about such things, but with us they are done every day. Come off with me, and see the race from the observation-train. I have one ticket, and I 'll get another—and you can send a message back to your sisters, if you like."

Trix's heart swelled with pure pleasure. She looked up to his face, and the bright tears in her eyes were contradicted by the smile on her rosy lips.

"I 'd go with you just as I 'd go with Jack," she said.

He left her with Mrs. Mordant, while he went to

send her billet to the yacht, and—a more formidable matter—to change his single place in the observation-train for two in one of its canopied cars, arranged, with ascending tiers of seats, to run by the river-side and follow the fortunes of the day. Falling in with a speculator who held elastic views of his possibilities in the matter of pay, Vyvan at last secured his prize, hastening away with a pocket as light as his heart— which did not prevent him from further investing, at an exorbitant rate of charge, in a bunch of the blue blossoms Trix loved, just arrived from New York in the oil-skin box of a florist.

"She 'd tread on these if the old grandfather had her at Mount St. Dunstan," he pleased himself by fancying. "Well, I 'll have to borrow, or foot it, to get back to New York to-night, and I 'll be hanged if I care which."

Long before the hour for the race, every seat in the observation-train was packed. Each car was a parterre of youth and beauty and bursting championship, crimson and blue sharing the space equally. Trix and her comrade, ignoring interruptions, talked to each other exclusively. By the best luck in the world, Mrs. Mordaunt and her party had also places in the car with Trix, and, with this triumphant assurance of security against criticism of the girl's stroke for independence, the young people abandoned themselves to enjoyment without alloy. But when, from the deafening tumult of the railway platform, the train finally moved off amid a blare of tin horns and rousing cheers, and they realized that the fateful hour was near, she grew a trifle pale.

12

"Courage," said Brock. "For Jack and Yale, remember."

"For Yale and Jack," said the girl, a big hysteric lump coming into her throat.

AND how fares it meanwhile with the brother Jack, for whom at least one heart in the vast multitude is beating as it never beat before? Let us leave the outsider's share of experience, which any one may have for the seeking—the sight of the river and its banks black with people; the thousands of craft anchored or swarming to the course; the blaze of color; the sound of incessant cheering; the strain of expectancy. Until the frantic moment of the start, let us have a glimpse at the crew itself. It may be that to look at a university boat-race from within the shell will give us a better understanding of what the achievement means to those who put their manhood into it.

During the last day or two before the contest, Jack has felt himself gradually inflating with strange excitement. He is no novice, and has rowed several good races at school, but they seem to him now to rate no higher than the mimic affairs in which he and Trix, in childhood, had watched their rival shingles vanish down the stream.

To be, in Freshman year, a member of the university crew, entitled to flaunt upon the breast of his shirt the coveted Y before envying classmates, has steeled the boy against hardship. He has borne cheerily the fortnight's ordeal in the white farm-house on the bluff above the Thames; the hard work in scorching suns, and long pulls on time, at dusk, over the storied battleground of the eights, and even the exasperating sarcasms of the great coach.

While older oarsmen have been grumbling at the monotonous diet of half-raw beef and eggs, varying roast chicken and oatmeal porridge, that has worn them down into so many healthy skeletons; while amœbean strains have arisen, hymning the rival charms of certain good black brier pipes, widowed since Christmas—Jack has exulted in pure animal spirits. He has nearly burst with pride on taking his place in the line of blue-and-black blazers, headed by the river-god himself, who march solemnly up to the quaint little house with broad eaves that flies the great crimson standard, to exchange solemn hand-shakes with the Harvard crew and its supporters.

Many of the red men Jack knows, and likes heartily. Several of them have been his predecessors in the boats at St. Peter's, but there is a strange constraint in their meeting here. He notes, with jealous zeal, what a fine-looking, fair-skinned set of thoroughbred stalwarts they are, oddly differing in exterior from the Yale greyhounds, and, in his heart, owns them worthy foemen. The two crews outdo each other in polite ceremonial. They ignore the recent spying with telescopes upon each other's movements in practice half-miles close in to the bank—and the gloom spread by reports brought back from his ambush in a single shell by a substitute clad becomingly in cotton tights with a stop-watch swung around his neck.

But now has come the day of reckoning. Jack has dreamed through the fever of the morning's wait, lying flat on his back in a darkened room, burning with thirst, and trying to heed a rough command to stir neither hand nor foot, his brain a kaleidoscope the while. They have been put on the water for half an hour, to make a final test of stretchers and new oars —the rigging a mathematical ex-captain and a skilful boat-builder have spent days in bringing to perfection; and after it have been sent inside, and bidden to rest. A hush as of a sick-chamber has hung over the place, until broken by the ruthless chatter of a party of girls, conducted by a non-boating graduate, to see the quarters of the crew. The men, prone inside, have listened sardonically to the little cries and chatter of these young women crowding in a tent upon the lawn, asking endless questions of the crew's interpreter, the flaxen-haired, gruff-voiced coxswain, who in his small person carries the dignity of the eight. Jack is just dropping off into a nap, when the quick summons of the coach is heard at the bottom of the stairs.

"Come, get up, you fellows! We're off in ten minutes. I've a word to say to you."

The lad's heart gives a bound, then seems to stand quite still. He is half dazed when they all meet below for a last injunction from the familiar voice.

"*Of course I think you'll win!* You don't suppose I'd have wasted my time here with you if I did n't. They 'll probably lead you the first half-mile; they always do, those red chaps; but—" here an expressive epithet—"you must go by them after that! Stroke, start her at thirty-six, and keep it up till you 're ahead if you die for it. You youngsters,"—casting about for a tremendous peroration,—"well, remember *I'm* looking at you!"

"Of course I think you'll win!" Like wine to the weary are these words from him who has always chided heretofore.

Embarked at last from the little floating stage near the start, one after another takes his place at the quiet word of the captain. In dead silence, every man shuts his teeth, and falls to thinking. Jack envies the phlegmatic country-bred fellow rowing at bow, who afterward avowed that he thought of nothing at all, and who is the best-conditioned of the lot.

With eyes strictly in the boat, unconscious of the thousands who gaze eagerly upon them, they paddle about for a few minutes, becoming gradually aware of their surroundings. Jack sees the flotilla of dainty, graceful yachts, and gives a thought to Trix, whom he believes to be aboard one of them. The long multi-colored observation-train lying off at a distance like a gaudy serpent he never thinks of as harboring his sister. He sees an enormous Sound steamer careen to one side with the weight of crowding passengers — the throngs of smaller fry, row-boats and launches, dogging their way.

And then a warning whistle from the referee's boat, as the busy little craft scurries to clear the course. Jack feels himself obeying the coxswain's order to straighten the boat out at the line.

Scarce a boat's-length to the starboard of them sit their rivals, engaged in stripping the jerseys from great muscles and mighty beef. At this spectacle the
    12*

young oarsman has a moment's sickly misgiving as to
results. But he looks ahead of him, down the line of
sunburned shoulders and lean, lithe bodies, and re-
members that here are stanch veterans of hard-fought
fights at school and college — heroes whose voices have
rung out over the mud of foot-ball fields, and on the
fatal third mile of many a tough four-mile pull in
rough water. And he is comforted.

Another whistle from the launch. Jack's brain is
void.

"Oars buried," almost whispers the cox.

Jack strains forward, and knows that the launch is
bearing close to them with a strange face in the bow.
There is a deathly hush.

"Gentlemen, are you ready?" asks the referee.

A pause that seems minutes.

"Go!" And they are off.

In the blank fear that he will do something wrong,
our youngster watches like a lynx the shoulders,
swinging back with mighty power at every stroke, of
the man ahead of him — that crewhile listless creature
who has been complaining of hard work, and watch
him now!

Mingling with the voice of the cox in his ears Jack
hears the swash of the other crew alongside, a bit
ahead, and the rage of battle comes into his soul.

"Why don't they quicken the stroke?" he thinks,
in his intemperate youth. "Oh! why don't we shake
'em off? Can we never pass those red chaps?"

There is Number 2 in the other boat. Jack yearns
to see him in the rear, and wants to do more than his
own share to bring this about. For the rest, he feels

blind and deaf, his brain opening and shutting in agony, his oar red-hot in his grasp. The stroke does quicken a point here, and the cox calls for an effort to go by.

The boat bounds under them, and the crew know the wild joy a sailor feels in danger from a squall, or a horseman on the rise of a high jump. They are rowing finely, their action magnificent, the stroke full, clear, and vigorous, a credit to the coach—"like a piece of well-oiled machinery," the reporters will write to-night.

Jack feels his muscles at work once more. Suddenly, above the shouting of the captains, and the swash of oars, he hears arise a cry—the war-cry of old Ironsides at Number 5. All the Yale boatmen know that cry. It is like the view-halloo of Drysdale in "Tom Brown," the dear old story-book that first made Jack a captive to the oar.

Now is the sweat of battle sweet in the mouth, and the ding-dong, hammer-and-tongs work has begun. Inch by inch they are gaining, and out of the corner of the eye the lad again sees Number 2 in the other boat. *This time he is opposite old Ironsides!*

The mile is past, and with the stroke's steady "Catch!" "Catch!" Jack knows, if nothing happens, they have won. He feels a pang of sympathy for that gallant other Number 2. Cheers ring out from the distant observation-train, cheers of "Yale!" "Yale!" and Jack again thinks of his proud little sister Trix.

"Βρεχεχεχέξ χοάξ χοάξ," comes in heavy unison from a steamboat. It is the chorus of Aristophanes's frogs adapted into a college war-song.

They have passed the navy-yard. His mouth is as dry as a kiln, but he is not exhausted. Hard rows and hot home minutes by the old Long Wharf in New Haven have seasoned him against that. He begins to think of the record. Can they touch it? The third-mile flag flashes by. The Harvard crew is a full two lengths in the rear, now, and the coxswain's note is a crow of victory. A cry is raised for a spurt at the finish. They are close in shore, out of the current. Wild shouts of joy come from Yale lungs on the train, its blue cars now plainly distinguishable, close at hand. And in the soothing dusk, shadows lengthening over the Groton shore, the Yale boat shoots across the line — victorious!

NEVER will Jack forget the mad rush of under-graduates tearing down from the still-moving train to heap congratulations on the eight, who sit as steady as posts, grinning comfortably, an oar's-length from the shore.

The Harvard boat is in, three lengths behind. One of their men has dropped over his oar, but is quickly brought to by a dash of water in the face. Their shell has been paddled out and across the river to the still quarters, where they will nurse their gloom, and dream of revenge next year.

There is no worthy partizan who cannot feel with a beaten crew, least of all the open-hearted fellows who have borne the burden, not of a day, but of six-months' labor and privation to show that they are men. The bulldog tenacity of that hard stern-chase has wrung

admiration for Harvard from the victors. "Ter qua-
terque ave, vincti," hear them cry.

Trix could not see for happy tears; but Brock, holding her hot little hand tight-clasped in his, told her
that all was well. He could distinguish Number 2
sitting straight, and no doubt as proud as Punch. The
Yale boat will go back to its quarters, and the men
repair to New Haven for such a night of such hero-
worship as it will stir their blood to remember while
blood runs in their veins. There is no chance for her
to speak with her brother, and she must try to be satisfied with present company. At which Trix gave the
speaker a look that freely told what he wanted most
to know.

The friendly shadows of eventide might have been
invoked to conceal the expression of the two young
people toward each other, except that nothing seemed
to call for apology just then. On the blue cars, people
old and young had been committing the most frantic
eccentricities, to be laughed at in cold blood afterward. Trix and Vyvan had merely, as the race progressed, drawn closer together, their pulses as one,
their breath mingling. When, for a brief space, the
bluff obscured the crews from view, Trix had made up
her mind that if, when they saw the course again,
Yale were behind, she would die upon the spot. It
was then that Vyvan had his opportunity to lean
down and whisper something in her ear—something
rash, unpremeditated, *squeezed* from him by the forlorn look of her face.

And then it was that Trix—fearless Trix, happy

Trix — threw away forever her chance to become joint-owner of the yacht *Incognita*, with all that it implied.

THE extraordinary conduct of Beatrix in running away from her natural protectors on the yacht was not the chief of Betty's troubles that eventful afternoon. She was even secretly glad that her younger sister had been spirited away. They had lingered long over the luncheon; many bottles of champagne had been called to a last account; fun, "as they found it" in Mrs. Shafto's set, had waxed noisy. Betty, who saw that Eleanor was wretchedly depressed, had to fathom for herself the workings of affairs. There had been, whoever was to blame, apparently nothing to find fault with in Hilda de Lancey's attitude, although Betty had no patience with Hildegarde's baby-ways, her low, appealing voice, her swimming violet eyes. One thing was clear — Jerry had to-day thrown off restraint, and was defying comment in his open flirtation with the enchantress.

As to that Sophy King or Shafto, Betty decided she was a snake in the grass, of the venomous variety. If Betty read human nature aright, she had worked upon Jerry's vanity to fan his old fancy for Hildegarde up to the present fashionable flaunting of a surface-infidelity to legal ties. Betty had many a time heard such affairs discussed as a matter of every-day in her society. Honest men and women laughed and joked over the like among their friends. To hold back from such jesting was to admit one's self provincial, crude — and Betty had not held back. She had enjoyed her own sallies on these subjects, and the way they were repeated and passed from mouth to mouth. But the dart had never before gone home to the bull's-eye of her innermost affections. She had watched Eleanor during this day of trial with increasing pain. It was evident that some especially deep wound had been sustained by the young wife, who bore herself withal so pluckily.

When the women left the table to the men, the two sisters went at once on deck, where the fresh air, and the lively spectacle of preparation for the race, brought a more cheerful look into Eleanor's wistful eyes. They talked of Beatrix, of Jack and his chances, with more of affectionate interest than jealous Trix had been willing to credit them with; and just as Betty was turning over in her mind how she might probe her sister's unspoken grief, Hilda de Lancey passed out the door of the cabin opposite to where they sat, and, accompanied by Jerry, walked forward to the far end of the boat, where together they leaned over the rail.

Nell saw, but did not look after, her husband. Betty, with a flash of feeling she could not govern, darted upon Gerald an indignant glance, which she knew from the expression of his flushed face and mutinous eyes would have absolutely no effect.

"Well, this is—" began Betty, at white heat.

"Don't, dear; I would rather not," interrupted Eleanor, her lip trembling a very little, but without giving other sign.

At this moment Mrs. Shafto came on deck, and, surveying the situation, drew a chair beside the sisters, and sat down with a fine air of *bonhomie*.

"Such a game of cross-purposes below," she said, laughing boisterously. "Timothy, who has found out your naughty little sister's prank, is in a big fit of the sulks, and Hilda, to placate him, had just asked, in her prettiest way, to be shown 'all over the yacht,' when, black as night with jealousy, as much as to say, 'Who's poaching on my preserves?' up steps Jerry, and carries off the prize—"

"You are speaking of my husband?" Eleanor asked freezingly.

"Bless me, whose else? But allow me to tell you, you don't play your cards well to-day, my dear. After your clever beginning with Theobald we looked for better things."

At this, Betty started violently. What Eleanor would have said was choked in her throat by the arrival upon the scene of Major Shafto, Van Loon, and another man or two, who, while puffing at their cigars, formed in a ring around the little group, ready to be amused at any cost. It was Mrs. Shafto's misfortune sometimes to miss her shot. To-day she had calculated well, and felt pretty sure of victory.

"We are discussing that little *tendresse* over yonder," she said easily, indicating to the newcomers, with an offhand gesture, the figures in the bow. "And I'm giving Mrs. Vernon 'points.' The fact is, American women are slow in following up their advantages, and after the compliment 'Slings and Arrows' paid her last week about the Theobald affair—"

"By Jove, Sophy, this won't do," said the deep bass voice of Major Shafto, who had been slowly taking in the scene.

"What won't do? Flirting with other people's property? You 'll have to make over society, old man, before you leave that out. Mrs. Vernon surely is aware that all the world has been praising her sharp practice in starting an opposition to Jerry's little game, though it was hardly to be expected in a disciple of the prudish Hallidays."

"I say! They 're in for it," whispered one of the men to Van Loon. "It 's a 'Ladies' Battle,' and we must stay and see it out."

For Betty, watching the malicious glitter come into Mrs. Shafto's eye, entered the arena at a bound.

"Don't stop your wife, Major Shafto," she said, with perfect self-command. "It 's so kind of her to show others the way she has won renown."

"That 's a nasty one!" added the previous critic, enjoyingly, in the ear of Timothy, who was growing rather scared.

"All of us, probably, except my sister, have read the paragraph Mrs. Shafto so delicately speaks of. And I don't believe there are many here who do not suspect its origin. But as regards the truth of it, I must really interpose. It is rather forcing my cards to make me announce my engagement in this way— but—I am only a woman, after all—I have promised to marry Mr. Theobald."

"Really? That does complicate the situation," said her opponent, with a daring laugh, and their hearers afterward declared that in spite of her evident discomfiture Sophy Shafto got the best of it.

"My dearest Betty, how glad I am!" Eleanor said, when the sisters were alone.

"I had no idea of telling yet — it is too new — only a week old. I can hardly believe it myself," Betty answered. "But the sight of that outrageous woman gloating over her mischief, and knowing that hateful little Leeds was within ear-shot, were too much for me. I did what I knew Tony would have wished."

"He is all that is kind and true," sighed Eleanor. "Oh, you will be happy, dear."

Unconsciously she emphasized the *you*, and Betty, bending over, kissed her affectionately. It had not entered into the mind of either to connect the date of Theobald's offer of his hand to Betty with that of the attack in print upon Eleanor's good name.

XIII

T has previously been told that the elder Mrs. Vernon's one authenticated link with established society was a certain Mrs. Vane-Benson, a far-away cousin of her late husband. This lady, also a widow, was well-looking and ambitious, and in her youth had married an Englishman of good family, whose death left her with a limited income, and with a daughter wedded for her pretty face by a rising barrister in London, who had frankly informed his wife that he could not abide his American mother-in-law.

When, therefore, Mrs. Vane-Benson visited London to be with those whom she styled her "dear ones," she was driven to the disagreeable necessity of taking lodgings near the daughter's house, and living in a "betwixt and between" way not at all to her taste. She knew "plenty of nice English people," but they could not be supposed to cherish active interest in an American who had no money to throw around. Her daughter's friends belonged to a young and gay set, and altogether Mrs. Vane-Benson felt the time in London hang heavy on her hands.

Oftentimes it had occurred to her to import the

family of some rich new American, and, for a consideration, to chaperon it through the London season;
but she was ease-loving, and this meant awful work.
The sudden wish of her cousin's widow to find companionship abroad had come to Mrs. Vane-Benson in
the nick of time.   It gave her courage, after engaging
the rooms desired at Claridge's, to take a neat little
victoria and drive around to see various friends, to
all of whom, over their tea-tables, she announced the
prospective arrival of a "ridiculously rich" relative
from the States.

It is most convenient that English people have no
curiosity about the social status at home of their
transatlantic visitors.   It makes the rough places
plain for so many worthy persons, and illustrates, on
English soil, the ideal American democracy.   Mrs.
Vernon, for instance, who in crossing the Atlantic
had been rather cowed by the stand-off grandeur of
one or two New York families of fashion who shared
with her the privilege of deck state-rooms and special
stewards, and ate and drank nothing that was not
served from their luxurious private stores, found the
same people in London mere diminished shades, herd-
ing at hotels, obliged to be content with paying their
way everywhere, and exhilarated by chance acquaintance with a baronet.   She, on the other hand, who
had so long languished without recognition in her
adopted home, was, by a series of fortunate incidents,
whirled with unexpected speed into the bosom of
Mayfair society.

The impelling cause of this was Mrs. Vane-Benson's
countess,—a stout, high-colored dowager who was

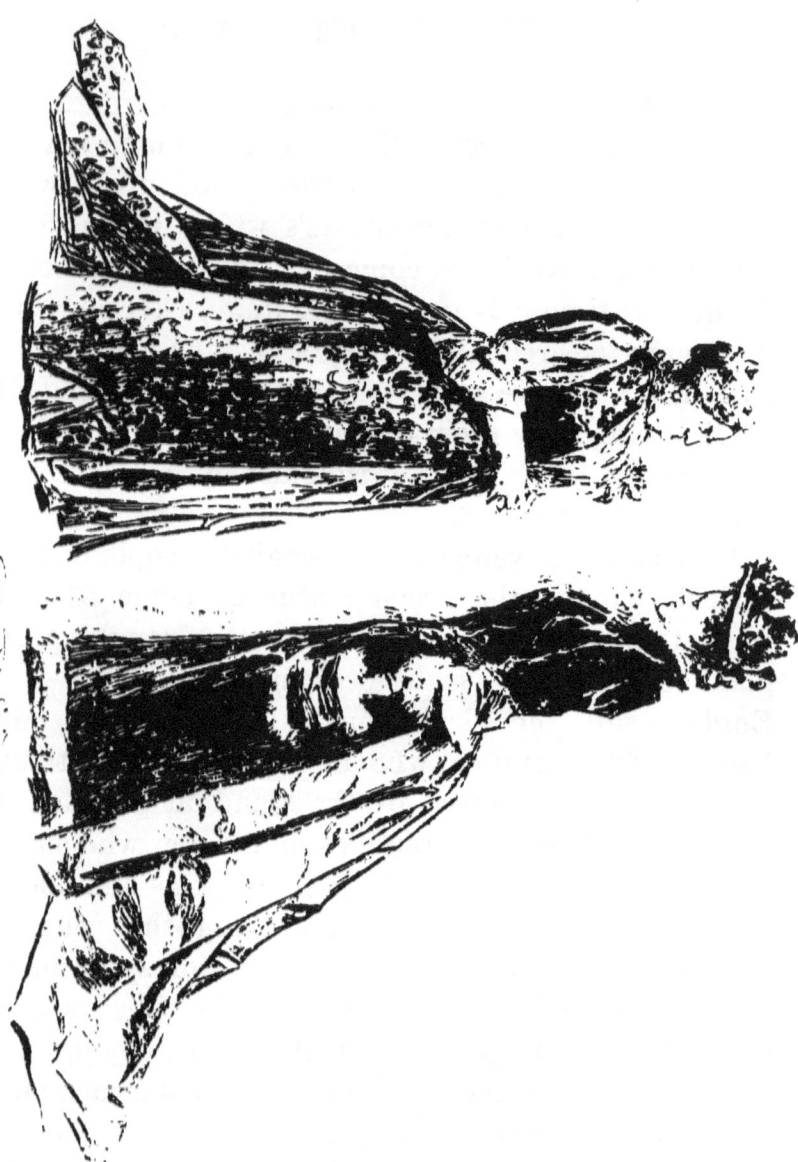

"YOU MUST TELL YOUR FRIEND NOT TO BE FRIGHTENED BY THE HOUSE."

fond of novelties, and had recently taken America under her wing,—who lived, when in town, in a narrow, dingy brick house in Curzon street, and spent her winters inexpensively abroad; the chief of those ladies to whom Mrs. Vane-Benson had gone at tea-time with her news.

It was Lady Shorthorn (or, to speak by the peerage, "Shorthorn, Dowager Countess of [Peer's widow]— Katherine Clementina Letitia Janet, dau. of," etc.; "mar. 1859 the 6th Earl of Shorthorn, who died 1870," etc.) who proposed to Mrs. Vane-Benson to remove her friend from the princely atmosphere of Claridge's into a private dwelling. It was her own son Lord Shorthorn's house in Prince's Gate, providentially to let for the season, or for two seasons, or for many seasons, if the price paid were sufficiently American. Mrs. Vane-Benson told Mrs. Vernon that poor Lord Shorthorn's wife had eloped under sad circumstances with one of his intimate friends, which would never have happened had her husband been able to keep up the house in Prince's Gate, since poor Lady Shorthorn could not abide the country in May and June.

Mrs. Vernon, acceding to all demands upon her purse, accordingly took possession of the Shorthorn residence, with its worn carpets, dull bedrooms, and drawing-rooms a wilderness of shabby chintz, sprinkled with ormolu candelabra, Dresden shepherdesses, and tarnished mirror-frames.

"You must tell your friend not to be frightened by the house," said the countess, unconscious of two meanings to her phrase. "I dare say it will seem formidable to her at first. And the servants may worry her—to have to have so many, you know. I'm told that in America you keep only two—help, don't you call 'em?—when you don't live altogether in hotels."

"Mrs. Vernon has been keeping more than two," said Mrs. Vane-Benson, meekly. "I suppose Lord Shorthorn won't mind her getting new chintz for the drawing-room?"

"If it's understood she's to leave it, no," said the dowager.

The new chintz, fresh paint and papers, balconies full of flowers looking out on the lovely square behind the house, Mrs. Vernon's talent for re-disposing furniture, and the objects of art that began soon to find their way to Prince's Gate, wrought in the interior a change to inspire Lady Shorthorn with sincere regard for the new tenant of Lord Shorthorn's house.

"Now she is settled, she must know somebody," remarked the dowager, who persisted in treating Mrs. Vane-Benson's compatriots as if they were all very young people of limited intelligence. "I have asked my son, when he has time, to call, and perhaps he may; but he is not enough."

"Lord Shorthorn must be so much at Ensilage with the dear children," said Mrs. Vane-Benson, although she saw the name of the nobleman in question repeatedly in the current gaieties of the "Morning Post."

"Oh, the children, of course. Three of them, or four,—yes, there are certainly four,—are a mistake for a man not yet thirty; but Shorthorn don't dislike being sometimes at Ensilage, though I always found the castle damp. The question is, How are we to get people to go to see your friend?"

"I had thought," said Mrs. Vane-Benson, hesitating, "of a ball."

"Hum! not bad," meditated the countess. "I think I could get people enough to come to a really good ball. But I should have to make her promise not to interfere."

"How not to interfere?"

Lady Shorthorn stared.

"To let me order things, and ask every soul who is to be there. I can't get into such a fuss as the duchess had with your Mrs. Central Parker last year. Why, the poor duchess had actually done everything, asked everybody, and expected it to be a really good ball. And then, what must your Mrs. Central Parker do, but take fright lest the duchess's people should n't come, and at the last moment invite a lot of her own friends! Of course the Americans all came. To be sure, the women were monstrous cock-a-hoop; but the duchess was so vexed, and has been telling everybody since that if it was a bad ball she washed her hands of it."

"Mrs. Vernon knows only a few of her country people in London — the Blanks and the Dashes," said Mrs. Vane-Benson, mentioning families of whom she felt secure.

"Oh, I have met your Mr. Blank, and he seemed to me a very nice sort of person, really," said the dowager. "I have met so few American men. Excepting that nice Mr. Black, who's just like an Englishman, and Mr. Blank, I don't think I know any. And, of course,

13*

there must be many more. To go back to the ball, tell your friend that I 'll do it, really, and she need not concern herself except to pay for it. Knowing the house as I do, it will be easier. Perhaps she will want to give the ball elsewhere; but I would n't care for that. She will enjoy seeing the ball the way I shall give it at Shorthorn's house. I 'm told all your best American parties are given at restaurants. It must be quite shocking, with strangers coming in and ordering their own food at the other little tables. I can't understand it in the least—"

"Oh, but you must let me explain to you—" cried Mrs. Vane-Benson, stung beyond the point of silence.

"—Or else you hire the whole floors of hotels, and take down the beds," pursued the countess, "and the guests go up in the—elevators. You see I know even your way of talking in America."

"The best way for you to know America is to visit it yourself some day," said Mrs. Vane-Benson, politely.

"Me? God forbid!" said the dowager. "We must have all one kind of flowers in the big saloon; fox-gloves, perhaps, or orchids—does your friend know orchids? And there must be plenty of champagne. Your friend must be made to understand beforehand about champagne."

"We drink champagne by the *gallon* in America," retorted Mrs. Vane-Benson in desperation.

"Oh, I think not," said Lady Shorthorn without a change of expression on her large, fair face. "It would make you so very sick. Lord Midlands himself told me when he dined at your—er—ah—chief palace, you know—the White House,—yes, a few years ago,—they gave him Apollinaris only, and handed boiled milk with the coffee, in large cups, during dinner. You see I 've made quite a study of America."

"I suppose when you get everything arranged for the ball," resumed Mrs. Vane-Benson, struggling no more, "it will be well to let the newspapers have a list of the expected guests."

"Perhaps; it don't signify—who reads newspapers?" said her ladyship, comfortably. "There are so many things in them one really can't believe. Imagine one of them saying, the other day, that your Mr. What 's-his-name had taken Guelph House for the season, and if he liked it, after staying here awhile, he would probably buy England. Now, fancy buying England—how could he, possibly? Tell your friend all I have said, my dear, and make her be most careful about receiving Americans till then, for there 's no knowing whether it might not spoil her ball."

THE ball, good or bad, was about to be an accomplished fact. Mrs. Vernon had been turning over her piles of acceptances, asking herself, with a delicious thrill, if it could be she—she whom the Van Shuters had so tardily recognized and the Van Loons had never invited—who was about to receive as her guests half the Lords Adolphus and Ladies Ermyntrude in the peerage.

The Shorthorn residence, from the hands of decorators astonished by liberal orders, had come forth a fairy-land of lights and garlands, draperies and plants. Late in the evening Mrs. Vernon, more excited than she had ever known herself to be, wearing a tea-gown of lace and satin, descended to the ground floor to bestow a survey upon her tables for supper, and the accompanying buffet.

At the moment of crossing the lower hall she had become aware of one of her footmen engaged at the front door in parleying with some would-be visitor, to whom he mechanically repeated the formula of "Not at 'ome." As she was returning to go again up-stairs, Mrs. Vernon caught a glimpse of what seemed a familiar face in the gap made by the partly opened door.

"*Hif* you please, 'm," said the footman, raising his voice to address his mistress with such emphasis that the powder flew from his ambrosial locks, "'ere's a pusson as won't by no means be hinduced to leave with-hout speaking a word with you."

He was a young footman, or what happened might not have been. The intruder, taking advantage of him to push by, entered the brilliantly lighted hall. Mrs. Vernon gazed at her—it was a woman—with absolute dismay. It was Calliope Jane Ketcham, once her companion "table girl" at Judd's!

"Mrs. Vernon, I believe?" said the new arrival. "Pardon me, madam, for seeming to intrude on you; but I am the London correspondent of the New York 'Planet,' and I have been instructed by cable to give half a column to your entertainment. If you would be so kind as to allow me to glance at the decorations, and at your list of acceptances—"

"You—I—please walk up-stairs," stammered the

unfortunate hostess, entirely at a loss for words or actions.

She led the way to the suite of glittering rooms above, fragrant with the breath of thousands of cut blossoms, and from which the last of the decorators vanished as they came in, bestowing upon Mrs. Vernon a bow as if to royalty.

"I guess I did n't do you much harm running you out o' New York, Luella," said Calliope's best-known tones. "'Pears like you 'd kinder think I was a blessing in disguise."

"You—torment! What do you want now?" almost hissed the lady of the house.

"Charming—acacia in that recess, I see," said the reporter, jotting down notes as a stray servant passed them by. "Now that I have a fair idea of the decorations, you will kindly allow me a glance at the gown you are going to wear? If you please, I will follow you."

In Mrs. Vernon's bedroom, the maids being absent, Mrs. Vernon's wrath broke forth.

"Go away! I won't stand it!" she said rapidly.

"Presently; all in good time, Luella. I am really a London correspondent, and this half-column means bread you would n't take out of my mouth."

"What has become of your gains from your last swindle in New York?"

"The last? Since circumstances forced me to withdraw from the 'Oppressed Wives' movement, I have been for a short time the widowed 'companion' of a lady whom you know. You can't think how I love

my weeds, Luella. They become me better than any
other dress, and people are always moved by hearing
of my poor dead husband. True, the lady I lived with
last was not so moved as she might have been by that
variety of sorrow. But her place suited me, and I
should have remained in comfort for the summer,
but at the end of a month I had to leave."

"Suddenly?" said Mrs. Vernon, with a curling lip.

"Suddenly," said Calliope, dropping her eyes, and
smiling. "But you don't ask me the name of my last
employer, dear. And yet, by a strange fatality, in
her house I found myself again involved in affairs
that had to do with you."

"With me? You 're mistaken there," said Mrs.
Vernon, with a hard laugh, all her society grace and
conventional mannerisms dropping from her like a
garment.

"With your son, then, whose habits and character I
had full opportunity to observe, for he was with her
every day."

"It is a slander. He swore to me—"

"Then you do know whom I mean. You are n't
surprised to hear that I went as guardian to the man-
ners and morals of the lovely Hildegarde? No, my
dear, don't interrupt me. As the boys at Judd's used
to say, 'I 'm the Wild Wolf from Bitter Creek, and
it 's my night to howl.' I found that young woman
has as neat a talent for double-dealing as I 've ever
chanced to see. No more heart than you 'd hold on
a pin-point, and a love of flirting for flirting's sake,
as other women love their drams of morphine and
chloral. Your youngster is a fool to think she

wants him except as a stop-gap till she can establish herself by another marriage. If she could get that rich fish Van Loon, she 'd soon give your Jerry the mitten. Meanwhile she likes playing with him, and dragging him on, and then shutting the door in his face. She 's no more pity for his wife than a cat has for a mouse. It 's been rare fun to her ordering him hither and thither, saying he must go to Newport because she means to take a house there, or to dear knows where, because she has a fancy for trying it. And, with all this, I don't suppose you doubt she owes *you* a grudge for not letting her become your daughter-in-law last year! And that Shafto woman is a match for her. When they 're not quarreling the two work together, and they 're together in mischief now."

"Do you expect only to make me angry by telling me of this?"

"Not at all," said Calliope, coolly, drawing an envelop from her pocket. "I pride myself on my system. I 've got a letter here that would open Jerry's eyes to Mrs. Hildegarde, and I want to sell it — *high*."

An hour later, Mrs. Vernon, girthed and buskined for the fray, stood at her post beside ample Lady Shorthorn, receiving such a crush of titled and distinguished personages as left no doubt in Lady Shorthorn's mind of her own cleverness in avoiding the disaster brought on the duchess by Mrs. Central Parker. There was not, all told, more than a handful of Americans in the rooms, and not a family among them that did not boast of the redeeming pretty woman. Late in the evening Lord Shorthorn strolled in, and was made known to his remunerative tenant.

Next day Mrs. Vernon awoke to find herself the fashion. True, a hornet's nest of gossip about her was let loose from the ignored Americans in London; but it was well on in the season, and by another year she would have lived such trifles down.

XIV

HE principal person, strange to say, to take umbrage at Mrs. Vernon's rapid rise was her original backer, Lady Shorthorn. One afternoon in July, when town was thinning fast, the dowager's one-horse brougham stopped before the house in Prince's Gate, and the dowager, going in, was encountered on the threshold by her son, who bowed to her, smiling, and hurried on to a hansom for which one of Mrs. Vernon's footmen had been whistling from the step.

Lord Shorthorn was a handsome young man, with a blond mustache, and legs so long that when he sat down they seemed to stretch interminably across the room. He was well dressed, from his shining hat and perfectly rolled umbrella, to the polished shoes upon his uncommonly large feet. Lady Shorthorn did not smile on him. She went at once up-stairs to the drawing-room, where Mrs. Vernon sat, and refused tea from that lady's hands, as well as bread and butter in thin slices from a large silver plate.

"I thought you would be leavin' town," she said. "Every one is leavin' town."

205

"I have the kindest invitations to Lord John's, and the Duke's, and those dear Cholmondeleys," said Mrs. Vernon, easily; "and I dare say I shall manage to do them all. But that is for August."

"You might go to—well—Eastbourne—for a while."

"Oh, I hate Eastbourne," said Mrs. Vernon, who, two months ago, would not have ventured to hate any place named by the dowager. "I have knocked about so much, I really like it better here."

"I saw my son goin' out of here. I am surprised he is not at Ensilage."

"Yes; every one says it is a most beautiful place."

"Beautiful in situation, yes; but damp, as I told you once before. I don't think any one living at Ensilage could long keep their health. And those three children—no, four, there are four—have their mother's temper; and I am obliged to say Shorthorn's own temper is—I told him so when they gave him his divorce—Shorthorn's own temper is dreadfully tryin', as any one who lives with him must find."

"Are you going to the Princess Argentine's garden-party at Lean Lodge?" said Mrs. Vernon, pleasantly.

"No; I 'm not asked—are you? Well, nothin' surprises one to-day. I suppose Shorthorn will be goin', too. I should think he 'd be careful about doin' as much as I hear he does. I believe it 's not generally known Shorthorn has a—er—a valve in his heart. Sir James warned him about it when he was quite a lad at Oxford."

"It is very sad," murmured Mrs. Vernon, looking at her with sympathetic eyes.

"LORD AND LADY WILLIAM HAMPSHIRE."

"He has undoubtedly a valve; and he has lived so fast, and got himself into such a ridiculous lot of debts, I don't know what's to become of him. The only hope we have is the marriage with his cousin Kelso's girl."

"Lady Sybilla is a charming person," Mrs. Vernon answered.

"It is so suitable; just what both families want. You will be interested, because you have a married son."

"Yes, I have a married son."

"Who must be nearly Shorthorn's age, is n't he? You know how you 'd have felt, if people had said he was goin' to throw himself away upon — er — ah — a nobody old enough to be his mother," said the countess, getting on her feet, losing her temper, and blurting out her words.

"Lord and Lady William Hampshire. The 'onorable Harthur Fitz-Greene, Sir Lionel Delacour," chanted a man-servant, withdrawing the portière.

"You will show Lady Shorthorn to the door," said Mrs. Vernon to this functionary, after greeting her new guests; and down-stairs puffed the large countess, in helpless, speechless wrath. She stepped into her brougham and drove away, feeling that she had not helped Lady Sybilla's chances, and registering a vow to have done with all Americans. Meeting Mrs. Vane-Benson in the park, she began by cutting that unoffending lady dead.

SOON after the onslaught of the irate countess, Mrs. Vernon was called, on her own account, to experience

14

certain pangs of anxiety regarding a son of whom other women took kind heed.

A few days later, when she was making ready to receive Gerald and Eleanor, who were due to arrive in Prince's Gate for a visit on their way to the Continent, came a startling note written by Jerry on the steamer and posted at Queenstown, telling her that he had crossed the ocean alone, leaving his wife with her mother in America—an arrangement of which he saw no definite prospect of change, and in consequence of which it would hardly be pleasant to meet his mother until feeling on the subject had had time to die down. He gave the address of a hotel in Paris where a letter from her might reach him, but warned her that no attempt at mediation would have a hearing from him, and that he meant to "travel till further notice."

Now, indeed, the world seemed for a while dark before the mother. But with characteristic energy she decided her plan of action, and, crossing by the night boat, was in Paris the next day, and early in attendance at the address given by her son.

Jerry, who at the most had expected from her an angry telegram or letter to which he would turn a deaf ear, as he had done many times before, was taken disagreeably by surprise. He received his mother sullenly, and she at once saw that he was under the influence of a mixture of emotions among which wounded pride was uppermost.

"Answer me one question, Gerald Vernon, or you are no son of mine," the widow said fiercely. "Has any other woman got to do with this mad performance of yours?"

"I don't know what business you have to ask," her
son said, "and I wish to heaven you 'd let me alone
and go away. I got a chill, or something, on that
infernal ship, and I have n't slept all night, and my
back and head are as heavy as lead."

"You do look ill," his mother said, struck, as he had
meant her to be, with sudden solicitude. "But, Jerry,
I can't rest till I know all. I 'm not going to appeal
to you for myself, or for that poor girl you 've left in
America, who 's worth twenty such women as you 've
let make a fool of you. I will change my question.
Where is Hildegarde de Lancey, who was a passenger
on the ship with you, as I saw by the published list ?"

"At a hotel, or on a train—or—how should I
know ?" cried he, stung into open answer. "It 's all
somebody's mischief. I 've not seen her since we
landed. She went up from Liverpool with a lot of
people to London on an earlier train, and left me no
address."

"She 's flying for higher game, Jerry, my lad," said
the widow, a satiric smile breaking upon her countenance. "She knows now you get every cent you have
from me; and she 's a deep one."

"Don't abuse her. I won't stand it," he cried violently, a dull red flush settling around his heavy eyes.
"She 's the best friend I have, and the noblest woman
I know—the only woman who understands me, and
gives me the sympathy I need."

"If that is your case, my dear boy," said the widow,
seating herself deliberately beside the lounge on which
he had cast himself, and taking out an envelop, "perhaps you will run your eye over this letter, written

recently by Hildegarde to her sister-spirit, Mrs. Shafto, and giving her frank opinion of a certain dangler at her apron-string. Don't ask me where I got it. It's *hers*, and that's enough."

THAT night Mrs. Vernon with her son re-crossed the Channel. They reached Prince's Gate for breakfast. But no consideration of the matin meal was of interest to Jerry, or would be so for many a morning to come. By the time he stepped out of the hansom, following his mother, the footman who came to take out the bags had to give him an arm across the pavement to the door, and within five hours Gerald was in bed, with a doctor and a trained nurse in attendance, in the first stage of a serious attack of typhoid fever.

XV

EN days before these things took place on the other side of the great Atlantic ferry, Eleanor Vernon in New York was joyously concluding her final preparations to go abroad with her husband. Their passage having been engaged in a ship leaving the next day, her heart was full of happiness at thought of what awaited her.

After a farewell visit to her mother's place on the Hudson, where the Hallidays were enjoying country life with their laurel-crowned hero Jack, she had come with her maid to town, to join Jerry at their own house.

Nell could not believe it was she whose spirit bounded with such delight at the prospect of putting the sea between herself and the old home. She was past reasoning. For so long she had dwelt upon this thought—if she could get Jerry away, off to herself, the happy time of their honeymoon would surely again return. Now it was soon to come; Jerry had ceased to vacillate, their plans were made, she was to taste of a deep, brimming cup of joy, Jerry's shortcomings

were washed away in a flood of new tenderness. No
need to go back to their sad days like the one upon
the yacht. Since Betty's engagement with Theobald
had been announced, Jerry had asked his wife's pardon
for what she considered his greatest offense against
her—asked in such manly fashion that her heart
melted with pleasure in yielding it. Mrs. de Lancey
and the Shaftos had gone on a cruise along the eastern
coast in Van Loon's yacht, and the young couple had
been perforce thrown upon each other for entertainment. During the visit to Eleanor's mother, they
had lived together for a brief restful time, and then
Gerald had been summoned back to town by Mrs.
Vernon's man of business, to consult about some of
her affairs.

It had been arranged between husband and wife,
their establishment being mounted for the summer in
picnic fashion, that he should take her for dinner to
Delmonico's. As the hot summer's dusk fell over the
dull streets, and Jerry did not appear, Eleanor began
to feel the pangs of her healthy appetite deadened by
growing anxiety. When Elsa brought up and pressed
upon her a tray of food, she made pretense of eating,
but, as the girl left the morning-room where she sat,
returned quickly to the window, and strained her eyes
into the gathering night. The gas-lamp near their
house, flaming out, seemed to mock her with dancing
in her tears.

Eight o'clock, nine o'clock, and a ring at the front
door. Eleanor, springing to the head of the staircase,
saw below a messenger boy's cap and uniform. The
note Elsa handed her was in an unfamiliar hand, and

once or twice she turned it over without opening, after the foolish fashion many people have of speculating about what can so quickly be ascertained.

Eleanor had had no previous experience with anonymous letters, and this, her first, was a bitter one. She could not comprehend why there should be no signature, and looked again ere she read the hateful lines that forced their way into her bewildered understanding. An older, wiser woman would have destroyed the note without reading, upon the first indication of its contents; but knowledge so to deal with the most cruel implements of modern social warfare comes only with experience. She was still clutching the paper, staring at what it told her, when her husband came into the room.

"Nell dear, you must have thought I was a wretch not to telegraph you I could n't come," he said, leaning down to kiss her. "But I was kept by a disagreeable thing: a man—an old college-mate of mine—got himself into a mess with drink and foolishness, and sent for me; and I had to haul him on his feet, and pack him out of town to his wife in the South. I'm just back from Jersey City, where I saw him to the train—why, what on earth is the matter, Eleanor?"

"It is not the first, but the most plausible, story you have made cover deceit to me," she said fiercely, facing him, and crumpling the paper in her hand. She lighted it above the lamp, and threw it into the fireplace, watching it blacken to tinder. "Oh, if I could only burn up as easily the shame my life with you has brought me!"

"Eleanor, are you insane? What is that letter?

What has put you into this state? Come, calm yourself. Are n't you well? Do you need a doctor?"

"There is no doctor who could help me," she said
drearily. "And I 'm not one to hide and equivocate
like you. I 'll tell you what the letter said—not all
—you may guess the rest. It said that woman—the
woman you still loved when you married me—is
going in the ship with us to-morrow, and that I am
the laughing-stock of all who know us."

Jerry was silent for a minute. He had fancied
Eleanor always the loving, pardoning creature she
had hitherto shown herself. He had absolutely no
conception of the hard scorn and anger now in her
face and voice. It drove out of him the soothing
words and kinder impulses he had brought up-town
to her, together with the truth upon his lips about
the cause of his detention.

"Oh! why is there no angel to stand by with a
flaming sword, and warn young girls what married
life is really?" she cried. "No one tells—no, not one
living soul—what we have to meet. The parents that
give us away, the clergyman that binds us, the books
we read, all lead us to the altar and leave us to our
fate! Who could dream of what I 've suffered in half
a year? And what help have I? None—God help
me—none!"

The burst of vehement indignation had dropped
suddenly into pathos, but Gerald was not moved.

"If you expect by this to make me fall down on
my knees, and own I 'm a wretch, you 're out of your
reckoning," he said frigidly. "There 's not one person
out of ten you could get to say you 're anything but

a jealous, hysterical girl. And what you hint about another woman I don't mean to notice further than to say it's the first time I've heard of expecting any one to overhaul a big ship's list, and say who shall or shall not sail in her."

"She is going, then, with us?" said Eleanor.

"With us? Certainly not. I am not so sure about our going at all, if this is the kind of traveling companion I'm likely to have. Mrs. de Lancey has decided to take her daughters and their governess to Switzerland for the summer; and *we*, as you know, intend to go direct to my mother's house in London."

"I will not go," she cried, with a swelling heart.

"Try to understand what you are doing," Gerald answered, after a pause wretched to both of them. "It may come to you too late to be sorry you made this stand against your husband."

Eleanor interlaced her hands, and her breath came panting. She looked at him with a wild appealing glance. He stood before her, determined, stolid, treating the whole affair like the outburst of a silly child. There was no sign of softening in his face.

"I refuse to go with you—and *her*," she said again, doggedly.

"Then you may go home to your mother, and ask her to teach you reason," he answered—and left her to herself.

SHE lay sobbing alone, all night, and early in the morning heard Gerald go out of the house. The hours wore on; men came and took away his luggage, already packed; and Eleanor, dreary and bewildered, felt as if each piece were a coffin carried down. By noon, shortly before the hour fixed for the ship to leave, she had made some excuse to her servants about a delay in their journey, and, calling a cab, drove in desperation to the steamer's wharf.

Even in the full air from the water she seemed to stifle as they drew nearer to the pier. Leaving the cab, she went, thickly veiled, along the passenger-way to the gang-plank, and stood for a moment behind a crowd of onlookers, gazing up at the thronged decks of the steamer. She had a wild idea that Jerry might even then see and know and want her; might beckon to her, and she would follow him to the death. But she did not catch a glimpse of her husband until after the warning gong had cleared the deck of visitors, and the little groups of passengers were beginning to congregate behind the rail to wave good-by to their friends on shore. At last, emerging from the throng, she saw him, alone, looking down as if searching in the crowd.

A keen delight filled Eleanor, and instinctively she darted forward with the impulse to fly up the gang-way and fasten upon his arm, never to leave her darling more. Just then a carriage drove swiftly up, intercepting her, and a party of belated passengers were hurried by the steamer's men on deck. They were a governess, two dainty, pretty children, and a beautiful blonde woman, her arms full of flowers.

A moment, and the gang-plank was withdrawn. The last mail-sack was hoisted on board, the last long-shoreman scrambled down his ladder bridge, the great steamer cast off from the wharf, and bore majestically down-stream.

As Eleanor went back to her cab, a gentleman looked after her, paused, looked again, and then hurried to her side.

"My dear Nell, what does this mean?" said Theobald. "Surely you were to have gone to-day. I came down at the last minute to see a friend off, and sought for but failed to find you in that extraordinarily genteel mob on board. Where is Vernon, and why have you changed your plans?"

"Will you drive up-town with me, Tony?" she said, under her mask of heavy gauze.

Seeing that something was amiss, he acquiesced without further query. When they were seated, and driving off, her head dropped on her breast, and she broke into gasping sobs.

"Oh! to whom can I turn, if not to you?" she said despairingly. "Tony, my heart is broken. He told me to go back to my mother, and—oh, my God!—what shall I do? He has forsaken me."

"The brute!" Theobald said between his teeth. He could hardly speak for the sudden violence of emotion she excited. It was not only the sight of the shipwrecked young life driven by storms back into port that moved him. In this moment of tenderness, the restraint of years was dashed away like a cobweb at a touch. He forgot himself, the time and place, his pledge to Betty; and the man's heart inside of him burst into fierce speech.

"Ah, let him go!" he said, hoarse and tremulous.

"You can be free. You can be happy. And I'm here to help you—I who'd give my life to save you tears like these."

Eleanor started and shrank as if she had been stung.

"This from you!" she cried wildly. "Oh, it is more than I can bear!"   ·

Then Theobald's brief madness passed from him, and he was filled with bitter self-reproach.

"Don't draw back from me, Eleanor," he said, striving to steady his tones. "Don't be afraid to trust me. Do I need to tell you that you are sacred to me? Let me take you to your mother; and I will go, and you need never look at me again. Oh, how you pain me with those eyes like some innocent creature's that I've shot to the heart! Speak to me, Nell, little cousin; tell me I am forgiven."

Behind this man's one offense there was a lifetime of unselfish tenderness; but, womanlike, she withheld from him whom she could never have loved the pardon always poured in full measure at Jerry's feet. Drawing the veil again over her face, she leaned back in her corner in silent anguish until her own door was reached.

When Theobald, who dared not offer to go in, awaited her instructions upon the threshold, she put her fingers into his faintly, coldly, and bade him good-by in accents barely audible.

"Then I may do nothing—save you nothing?" he pleaded, cut to the quick. "You dismiss me without pardon, or hope that I may come to you again?"

"Not now," she answered, in a voice he would not

have recognized as Nell's; "but it is not that I don't believe in you. Go, please." And she passed away from him.

THE day wore to its interminable close, and Eleanor had beaten about in a dreadful circle of indecision as to what course to pursue. One thought was dominant —she must try to hide from those who loved her the wrong done her by him she loved. Among all the people who had been her friends and intimates since childhood there was no one to whom she could bare this bleeding wound. Theobald, almost her brother, would have been the first to occur to her, and he— Eleanor's face flushed hotly with the remembrance of that shock.

What was right? What was best and truest to Jerry and to her higher self to do? It might be that she could find still in town the rector who had offici- ated at their marriage, and who had held her in his arms at the baptismal font; and stealing from the house, she walked, veiled as before, through the cool of evening to his home.

"Would the rector see a lady for a moment only?" was the message she sent in, waiting with an odd sense of the change from her position of command and influence wrought in her own mind by the cause of her present visit.

She sat, trembling, and was presently relieved, in a degree, by the appearance in the room of the rector's wife.

"If you will tell me your errand, I will speak to my husband—" she began, peering curiously at the stranger, and when Eleanor, lifting her veil, came forward, uttered an exclamation of jocular surprise.

"Nell Vernon! Why, child, who could suppose it was you? If you knew the watch I have to keep on ladies who visit the doctor! They take up so much time, and worry the life out of him with their fads and fancies. Men are men, and the clergy are human, though the laymen never make allowances. The way the women hang upon my good man's words—no wonder he 's a little short when we contradict him at home sometimes. And they tell him everything, from quarrels with cooks to spats with husbands. The truth is, child, he is dressing to go out to dinner, and if I will do as well—some of your 'Girls' Lodging House' business, no doubt."

"What I had to say need not disturb him now," said poor Eleanor, quietly moving toward the door.

"Then you 'll call again, or write? I heard you were going to the other side. And how 's that handsome husband of yours, my dear? My girls are just wild over him, but I believe all women are. Take my advice, and don't let him flirt too much."

"I ASKED for bread, and ye gave me a stone," the girl murmured involuntarily, as she found her way again into the street, and the crushed spirit that had yearned to be made whole by the healing touch of God's pity expressed through his minister was sent out unhelped to wander stumbling in the night of its despair. She looked down the vista of a side street, and knew that it ended in the river.

"When a tie like ours is wrenched apart, and there is no help, death were sweet and merciful," she thought, staying her steps for a confused moment upon the curbstone of the crossing.

Then two girls, accompanied by a young man, walked by her, laughing lightly. The voice and manner of one of them put her in mind of her sister Beatrix, and instantly the claims and duties of her life of every day rushed back to take possession of the distracted citadel from which grief had temporarily dislodged them. With the thought of Trix came that of the girl's happy young love, just now on probation with the authority at home, and Eleanor was cheered by it as if a warm hand had taken her frozen fingers into its clasp. It roused in her human interest, and melted the hard resentment against Fate that had begun to glaze over her sympathies, and that made her forget the world contained others than Jerry and Hildegarde.

Unconsciously she quickened her steps in the direction of her home, but, at the corner nearest it, stopped again, overcome by the thought that her servants, already in possession of an evening paper, might see, perhaps, some announcement that Jerry had gone without her, and thus her miserable pretense of a delay would be exposed. How could she face Elsa's smooth civility, veiling the servant's galling knowledge of a domestic skeleton? Oh, for brief respite from the humiliation of public comment or sympathy!

To-morrow—there was no help for it—she would be forced to go back battered and bleeding to her mother's home, carrying her shame to be shared by those tender hearts!   But now, ah, now—only to escape another night in her desolated home!

The image of Gerald's aunt, the avoided and isolated Miss Tryphena, presented itself in sudden invitation. Eleanor, hastily, lest she should repent, retraced her steps to the avenue, and got into an omnibus bound up-town.

The long, jolting expedition gave her time to reflect on the temerity of expecting sympathy from the source she sought.   Of the passengers who climbed in and dropped out of the vehicle along its route none were known to her; for the society element of town was off on its annual hejira, and people who remained within its limits were of the fraternity of workers. She found herself studying the faces of these strangers, eagerly wondering if their hearts carried a dead weight like her own, envying the couples who were bound together to their homes, envying the gossips who sat, knee to knee, gaily discussing important trivialities.   And when a young woman, laden with parcels, gave her hand to her husband, who helped her to descend, beaming on him with a transparently loving smile, Eleanor turned away fretfully, and wondered if she should never reach her goal.

Aunt Tryphena's house, one of sad brownstone exterior, in a long, forbidding block of buildings from which it varied not a whit, was inhabited, and her butler, in coming to open the door, stopped on his way to light the gas in the hall from a fixture like a shepherd's crook.   This homely sign gave Nell courage to send up her name to the mistress of the castle, who, if an ogress, lived in the conventional way of other householders; and at once Miss Tryphena descended to her long drawing-room swathed in gray linen coverings, and illumined by a single jet of gas.

"I was bitten by a mosquito here last night," she said severely. "Edmunds knows I told him to keep this room quite dark. There is light enough from the electric globe across the way." And, to Nell's satisfaction, the offending luminary was at once put out. "Now, you will tell me, if you please, what brings you here when the soup is just ready to be sent up. Unless Jerry's in jail for debt, or Luella's married, I can't imagine what you can have to say to me."

"Oh, Aunt Tryphena, be kind to me," cried the girl, seizing one of the old lady's large, rough hands in both of hers, and bursting into bitter sobs that could no longer be controlled.

"Do?" said the spinster, when, the belated soup discussed, and dinner over, the two resumed their talk. "There, child, you look like a human being, not a ghost, now you are fed, and have had a glass of wine. Why, there is but one thing to do. I will go downtown first thing to-morrow morning, and engage a room in the quickest steamer we can get for Saturday. I will take you straight to London, and leave you at Luella's house before even your mother has had time to find out the condition of affairs. And I will then catch the first boat by the Dover-Calais route, and go to a place in Switzerland I left three years ago. It is a place that suited me exactly, but I could n't stand a pair of esthetic idiots from England

15

who were stopping there, who used to complain of the sunsets because they were too crude. Now, write a line by Edmunds to your maid, and have some things sent here for the night, as it will be lonely for you in that house, and cheer up, child, for Heaven's sake, for I could never abide to have anybody complaining but myself."

" But, Aunt Tryphena," said Eleanor, a crimson tide overwhelming the pallor of her face, " even if Jerry is there, I ought not to—should I?—thrust myself upon him. Oh, did n't I tell you how he cast me off, and killed my love?"

" For better, for worse, child; you must remember that for both of you," said the old woman, with a break in her gruff voice. " Whatever comes, you will have been true. And your love 's not dead; don't think it. Keep it alive,—breathe new breath in it,— it will make this struggle strengthen you. And, as certainly as I live, if anything will bring him back to you love will."

" Back from another—oh, no, no!" cried Eleanor, tortured by the thought.

" My dear, it is for you to choose. But I think you 'll find your jealous miseries have exaggerated things. The chief offender is that De Lancey person, backed up by your 'best society.' Jerry 's had the bad luck, from all I hear, to fall into the hands of a woman who has the consciousness of disappointed schemes to help on her love of coquetry. It 's not a common experience you 've had to bear so early in married life — even among what I call the most friv- olous and brainless set of people on this continent.

But that creature will continue to go at large, and ruin other homes, no doubt. Our boy 's weak, but he 's not all bad. If his father had n't had the misfortune to die and leave all that money in the hands of a silly woman, Jerry Vernon would have been, as men go, a fair sort of man; I don't suppose you know, or he cares, but the fact is I loved Jerry dearly when he was a boy. I thought he would grow up to be—but that 's neither here nor there. In my opinion, it is for you to straighten out this snarl. If you think enough of an old maid, tough as a nut, who 's nobody's friend, to take advice from her—don't let the gulf widen, don't let your husband go without stretching out your hand to bring him back. Come with me, Eleanor, and leave your pride behind."

There was silence for a moment in the shadowy room, and the sound of a woman's short, quick, gasping sob; then Eleanor

Smote the chord of Self, that, trembling, pass'd in music out
    of sight.

"I will go," she breathed, and with a sudden movement cast herself upon Aunt Tryphena's neck, and let the delicious cordial of new hope warm the sad current of her widowed heart.

Two years have passed since the green shades of the widow Vernon's marble palace in the higher regions of Fifth Avenue first proclaimed that lady out of town. The wide portal is boarded over, and the premises are in charge of an Irishman and his wife, whose frowsy children gambol behind the basement windows, and skate on rollers over the asphalt of the adjacent street. Above the area level all is silent, gloomy; and as yet there is no hint that the mistress of the palace will resume possession.

From within doors the best of the bric-à-brac and pictures and books, with the portraits of Gerald and his mother, since admired at the Royal Academy, were long ago taken to be boxed and expressed to the domicile in London, where the dowager Lady Shorthorn has not yet called upon her son's recently made wife. The American Lady Shorthorn can, however, afford to be indifferent to this blow of Fate, as she is already a social power in her adopted home, and as her young husband, upon whom she has settled a liberal income, in addition to paying his debts, makes an attentive and good-humored spouse. She is also on excellent terms with her son Gerald and his wife, who, of course, spent all of that summer at her house while he was convalescing from the long attack of typhoid through which Eleanor, arriving just in time from America, nursed him so devotedly. And the new countess ("Martha Louisa Anne, daughter of Colonel William Judd, United States Army, U. S. A."—you will find her recorded in Burke and Debrett and Dod) has had lately the satisfaction of refusing a card (requested through a friend, for her world-famous ball) to a Mrs. Van Loon of New York, who has been stopping at Claridge's.

Mrs. Calliope Jane Ketcham is at present in one of her periodical states of eclipse. When and where she may next appear it is impossible to predict, but my Lady Shorthorn will, no doubt, be among the first to ascertain.

Miss Tryphena Vernon, not in the least like the crusty benefactor of the novelist who, under the impulse of a good action in the last chapter, reforms and remains angelic ever after, would probably take the head off any inquirer as to her relations with her niece and nephew. But Nell knows that they are affectionate, and both she and Jerry submit to be hectored by the old lady in grateful memory of her influence at the crisis of their married life.

Nell's home people suffered, as may be imagined, from the strange reports that were set afloat at the time when Gerald left his wife to follow him across the ocean. But although slander did its best, nothing was fixed upon any participant in the affair, beyond the fact of "some foolish quarrel between the young couple about Hilda de Lancey, who it was well known was chaperoned on that voyage over by the Blanks and the Dashes," and, it was equally well known, meant nothing serious by her little flirtation with Jerry Vernon, now said to be "the shadow" of his wife.

And so even Mrs. Halliday, her other daughters, and her son knew little of the darkest chapter of the young wife's experience. In the autumn after these events Nell's mother and sisters joined her in Paris for a fortnight before the Vernons set out for their winter's journey in the East, and, during that time, satisfied themselves that the first year of her married life bid fair to round itself peacefully to a close.

The wide old Halliday house in New York, facing the railed square on the eastern side of town, and noticed by passers for its growth of wistaria looped between the chimney-tops in great ropes tasseled in

spring with purple under a mist of greenery, is forever deserted by its former occupants. For months
workmen had it in their hands, coming and going
between piles of brick and mortar encumbering the
street.   Its front has been transformed with plate-
glass windows and gilded balconies.   Within marble
halls, a buttony page keeps watch where once old Andrews came creaking to open the front door.   A prosperous club has taken possession, and the Hallidays
will be known in it no more.

Beatrix, who was, after all, the chief sentimentalist
about this change, is supplied with a fount of private
happiness that enables her to rise above minor con-
siderations of every material kind.   In her eyes, as
in those of his mother, to whom and his grandfather
Trix will one day go for a visit when the roses are in
bloom, Brock Vyvan is a "man of to-morrow," as to
whose future there can be no doubt.   Betty's marriage
with Mr. Theobald occurred upon her return from
Europe.   And Jack, for whom the four years of college
life leave the imagination no room to vary occupations, is still at Yale, holding the blue banner man-
fully as he ascends.

A piece of news that afforded almost a fortnight's
gossip for the fashionable world was the marriage of
the heir of the Van Loons with Mrs. Hildegarde de
Lancey, "privately," at Nice.   Betty Theobald says
the fur has not ceased to fly in the Van Loon family,
but then, as Mrs. Van Shuter would observe, everybody knows how Betty Theobald will talk.

The other home in New York in which we have
been called on to take passing interest—Eleanor's

first nest, fitted up for her occupancy with such lavish
love—remained for a time vacant after Mr. and Mrs.
Vernon set out for their two-years' wandering.   In
January an agent had orders from Lady Shorthorn to
find for it an occupant, and succeeded in placing there
the Hempstead Hunters, who take a different house
every year, but are in demand as tenants because they
are conscientiously childless, and dine out six nights
in the week.

And so—fortunately, if temporarily—our young
couple have dropped out of the society that claims
them for its own, and that came so near breaking the
bond it once assembled to applaud.   In the companionship of their nomadic existence, each has learned
dependence on the other; and the irresistible habit
of married life has had time to weld their chains.
Already they have learned to look back upon that
early ordeal, bitter though it was, as an episode that
may be forgotten in the memory of happier days.

www.ingramcontent.com/pod-product-compliance
Lightning Source LLC
Chambersburg PA
CBHW020119030726
47498CB00006B/2173

* 9 7 8 3 7 4 3 3 0 5 2 7 4 *